Disclaimer

Divi and Ankleshwar are real places that are most certainly located in Gujarat. But, in this novel, they bear no resemblance to the actual towns. All the characters are products of my imagination and all the situations are fictional. Any resemblance to living people is entirely coincidental.

Around the world with four samosas

Pravesh Jain

ISBN 979-8-88641-514-8

Contents

Preface

Genuine literature powerfully captures the experience of life. It explores various aspects and modes of human activities on the one hand and, on the other, expounds them through multiple stories, situations and events that go into the making of a panoramic view of the world at all levels of the human condition.

A writer is one who is driven to provide an outlet to all the impressions of the external world that impinge upon their consciousness and then, in a subtle way, spread out through their entire being. Whatever is churned in the deep recesses of the writer's sacred self takes on the form of a literary work. It acts in two ways: it gives pleasure to the creator—the author—and it also gives pleasure to the reader. Viewed from this angle, the writing of a novel is a mind-boggling occupation. It involves high-level, complex creativity.

It is my conviction that the primary function of a novel is to give pleasure by presenting before the reader a cogent and sensitive portrayal of life in its diverse forms, each with its inherent opulence. The novel should not aim to teach through sermons and precepts. If it does so, then it is a total disaster.

Around the World with Four Samosas is one such effort by me. I was inspired to write it when I read about the chance meeting, on a train, between a brilliant IIT graduate and a semi-literate *samosa* maker, and how it had disillusioned the former, the person with the superior education and more privileged background. The humble *samosa* maker turned out to be a financial wizard within his own ambit of activities. Reading about this gave me a new view of life. India is full of talented people working in different fields. A revolution is possible if we create a bridge between trained and sophisticated minds and untrained creativity.

This novel has tried to portray this view through its two protagonists: Vivek, a highly sophisticated professional, and Paresh, a *samosa* maker. The association between these two creates a new sensibility and provides a glimpse into the "new India" and its infinite possibilities. The book is sure to motivate those who are willing to walk in uncharted areas and bold enough to seek and pave new avenues for themselves.

The rest is for the readers to decide.

– Pravesh Jain

A Chance Meeting

He got on the train. It was crowded, but his berth was reserved. He was very disturbed. The events of the past few days had unfolded at such a rapid pace that he had not had the time to absorb them and realize that his life was never going to be the same again. It struck him when he boarded the train that he had lost everything. There was no going back. Now he had decided to undertake an unplanned journey into a foggy future. Much like a drifter, a man without any purpose. So unlike what he used to be.

Family, friends, acquaintances, familiar paths—all of it had been strange to him and he had often wanted to run away from all the strangeness surrounding him. But now, things had taken a form that had pushed him to turn his desire into a decision.

The trouble had been that he was not sure where to go. If at all he left, he used to think, it would be at the cost of being called an escapist and irresponsible loser. Now, things were different. He felt the time was right for him to chart unexplored terrain, in the hope of finding some peace and purpose in life. He wasn't the impulsive sort, but he took this decision on a whim, because this was the only way out that he could think of. He left with a trunkload of confusion and doubt and very little possibility of being able to find answers to the many questions clouding his mind. Yet, even in this desperate situation, he held on to a beacon of hope—the promise of something new.

Clothes, books and a few miscellaneous articles were his only companions. Although he had told his mother at home that he had signed up for a meditation course somewhere far away and would be gone only a few days, deep down inside, he knew he would not be coming back to his previous life ever again. After the death of his father and the break-up of his own marriage, his mother was a distraught soul. It pained him to see her, once a dominating lady who had held her own through all the ups and downs of life, turn into a silent, lone and aloof figure.

Maybe the world has its own ways of telling us that we can't live the same life all the time, he thought. Maybe it was time for him to embrace change and just go with the flow rather than swim against the tide. Life demanded that he go away and he was submitting to it. Informing his mother of his unplanned plans was his duty and he felt relieved at having at least fulfillled it.

He arrived at the railway station thinking of travelling to some unknown and remote village. It would not just calm him down but also provide an escape from the demons of the past. He had had enough formal education to know that such escapes sometimes had a great healing power. This was why he wanted to lose himself in the solitude of some unknown place, a place where he could brood over his failures, be one with his soul and, if possible, start living life all over again.

Since his childhood, he had been shy of demonstrating his emotions and sentiments. He felt that displaying emotions was an attribute of the weak. He had the practicality of his mother and the strict demeanor of his father. This was a trait that he had inculcated with some deliberation but mostly in a subconscious manner, to suit what he thought was his parents' preference. He was rather proud of being the soulless person he had become because that, he thought, would make his parents proud of him and make them accept him happily. Since both his parents felt that feeding him worldly wisdom rather than making him a social animal would prove beneficial for him in the long run, he agreed to be like clay in their hands, often just to get them off his back. He chose to drift with the current, much like he was agreeing to go with it now. At an individual level, he would have wanted to be a completely different person, but as part of the family he was born in, he became one of them. Now that he was feeling the need to live his life the way he wanted and to emerge as an individual, he had taken the first step: leaving behind his house and everything for the unknown. Was he demonstrating traits of rebellion or was he just ready to come into his own?

He had booked himself a ticket for Pune. At the back of his mind, he had thought of spending some time in a *vipassana* center there and with Rammo, his nanny, who had settled in the city. He already loved the unpredictability built into his journey. He felt like Indiana Jones embarking on an adventure to an exotic land in search of discovery. Finding his berth, he sat down quietly.

But calm was not to come.

Across his berth, he noticed a rather talkative family. He felt instinctly then that his journey was going to be a very difficult one if he was going to have to spend all of it in the same compartment as this family. He silently wished that the T.T.E would come to his rescue by announcing that the family had occupied the wrong compartment and that they were required to move to the next one. How he wished for them to vanish and leave him alone with his thoughts!

The family was chatting away animatedly, much to Vivek's discontent. He had no choice but to tolerate them. *After all, they are in my compartment, not my life,* he reasoned, and prepared himself to enjoy the journey as much as he could under the circumstances.

He noticed that, even though the family was noisy, they were a compact lot. There was the typical Indian husband, the one who would be at the helm of affairs and taking control of everything around him to make sure his family was at ease. He had sharp, green, piercing eyes that were incongruous with his tan skin, but otherwise his looks were nothing to write home about. Then there was the archetypal Indian housewife. She was submissive to her husband's demands to keep the decibel level under control when talking to him, but a woman on a mission when warning her two teenage children to behave themselves. She was voluptuous, with curves in the right places, and, draped in a sari, could have easily passed herself off as a woman in her mid-twenties rather than the mother of two teenage children. Both the kids seemed to be restive sorts. However, in spite of their squabbling, they had a quiet charm, too. *A typical Indian family*, Vivek thought to himself. Although they lacked studied sophistication, they appeared happy and content. They were definitely connected with each other despite their varied temperaments. A feeling of ennui overtook Vivek as he closely observed the family. All of a sudden, he felt something was missing inside him. Perhaps the sight of a happy and loving family was too much for him to digest. Unable to concentrate on his thoughts because of the constant cacophony of sounds around him, he decided to just let himself be and accept that the family would irritate him until the end of the journey.

Since there was still time for the train to begin its journey, he decided to get down and treat himself to a little snack. He bought himself two *samosas*, the popular Indian fried savouries filled with a delicious mix of boiled potatoes, dry fruits and spices. He found the coriander chutney accompanying his snack rather tasty, unlike anything that he could recall. For a while, he was happy to have disassociated himself from his noisy neighbours and be on his own, but it was not to last. The train's horn went off, signaling that it was time to go back and share his compartment with the people he had chosen to dislike at first glance. But something as simple as the yummy taste of the *samosas* and the tangy chutney kept him in good spirits.

Sitting at the window seat had its own advantage, Vivek soon discovered. As he gazed outside at landscapes that were receding and being taken over by new ones, he was transported into various stages of his life, away from the distractions of the strangers surrounding him.

Reflecting on incidents from his childhood, his thoughts slowly began to meander through his unpleasant relations with his parents and sister, his life in college and his unhappy marriage and relieved acceptance of divorce, all of which had led him to this train. He was soon in a world of his own, where past moments were the only companions he recognized.

Vivek came from a socially and economically well-to-do family. His father, a chemical engineer by training, owned a small empire of chemical dyes, which he ran along with his brother. His mother, though an architect by qualification, had transformed into a social activist of sorts—she was more interested in freeing the world from its problems than in looking into what exactly was going on in the lives of her two children.

From early on, Vivek had felt the pressure of having to be and become something his parents wanted, rather than what he would have liked. Entrusted in the care of his grandfather, who was a strict disciplinarian courtesy his army background, Vivek was taught to be tough and practical in life. His grandfather had left his own father's family business and joined the army because of his inherent need for discipline and order—in his opinion, the forces were the best place to learn to be tough and practical.

One particular incident he remembered vividly from his childhood also formed the foundation of the characteristic he later in life became imprisoned with. It was simple. He had expressed to his grandfather the desire to become a musician. His grandfather had become furious. His mother had come to everyone's rescue and given him a slap that still resonated. His desire was destroyed once and for all. Simple.

His grandfather had asked him, "What do you plan to become in life when you are all grown up?"

"A musician," he had said.

His grandfather had laughed his head off and said rather mockingly, "A musician?! Well, you don't have very bright future prospects then."

"But why, Dadaji? I love playing the guitar and the piano and I enjoy music class the most. I feel so free. The sound of the flute soothes my mind and I feel there is no worry in this world," he had insisted innocently.

"Worries! And what possible worries do you have at the tender age of 11? Young folks like you should bother about nothing but studies. For you, the aim should be to become an engineer so that you can help your father and uncle to take the business forward," his grandfather said authoritatively.

Vivek, dismissing his grandfather's attempt to control him, replied, "But I don't like science. It gives me a headache. I like music more. Besides, I'm a young man now and I can think for myself and decide on my own what I want to be in life. I don't want to talk to you if you aren't ready to share my ideas. And I remember you went against your father and joined the army."

Listening to these protests caused Vivek's grandfather to become agitated. He couldn't fathom a grandchild, supposed to be a child forever, speaking this way. What he, a senior citizen, had done as a youngster was his business, not to be brought up by a mere chit of a boy.

Vivek's grandfather had been the final authority in the house and, no matter how liberal the rest of the family were, without his consent and permission, not a single thing would move in the household. After all, he was the head of the family and he had to find some meaning in it!

In Vivek, his grandfather saw signs of rebellion. He was caught off-guard by his own grandson threatening his position in the household.

"For years, no one in this family has dared to challenge my decisions. Who do you think you are to change that today? Your father and uncle studied engineering because I ordered them to do so. They did as I instructed and you, too, shall follow suit and do what I have told you right now. I don't want to hear another word on this. Now go back to your room and study. And science it must be!"

Seeing his grandfather's temper hit the roof, Vivek wanted to run away, but discovered that his legs had turned to jelly. The moment was frozen. He had frozen. Hearing the booming voice, Vivek's parents came rushing to the living room. Vivek was standing before his grandpa with his head lowered, totally stunned.

"What happened, Papa? Why are you so angry?"

"Ask your talented son what exactly happened. I'm sure he is grown up enough to explain the entire situation to you."

"Vivu, your grandfather is saying something. Why don't you expain yourself?" came Vivek's father's stern voice, cutting through the heat in his ears.

Before Vivek could open his mouth to say anything, his grandfather said, "Your son wishes to become a musician when he grows up! Can you believe that? He doesn't think being an engineer would suit him because he doesn't like studying science. And what good can a person playing the guitar or tabla do in life? Ask him if his musical instruments will pay him to even feed even himself, forget his family. Adarsh, I am telling you in advance, your son has fallen into bad company. His friends are polluting his mind. Control him now or you will soon lose him to his despicable desires."

Vivek's father, Adarsh, was a practical man and mirrored his own father to a great extent, but had always been gentle when it came to his son. He had been a loving father and Vivek had always looked up to him.

At that moment, all Adarsh could say was, "But Papa, he is just a child, still at an impressionable age. His desires and wishes will change with each and every passing day. I guess it is a bit too early for him to make up his mind and decide what he really wants to become in life. I'm sure he must have seen some rock star on T.V. and must have thought it to be the best way to lead life. There is nothing to worry about. Right, Vivu?"

Having gotten the sense that at least his father was around to console him, understand him and take his side, Vivek had grown confident enough to speak. He replied, "No, Papa, I really do want to become a musician. It has got nothing to do with watching anything on T.V. I love music and want to pursue it as a career."

These words, blurted out with intense fervor, seemed to pierce through all that his grandfather stood for and he again lost his cool. He boomed, "See, I told you! Your son has gone mad. He doesn't just wish to be a musician, he has decided also to give up all other things in life for its pursuit. Now can you understand what I'm saying?" He raised his voice a little more and, with an all-knowing look, continued, "Look, he has no respect for his elders. He is now going to tell us what is to be done. I'll not tolerate such indecent behavior in this house! I'm warning you, Adarsh, you either tell your son to forget about his plans or all of you be prepared to face the consequences."

Vivek's grandfather wielded full control in the household, including over the finances, even though the sons were the ones going out into the market and applying every strategy to expand the business. He was a shrewd and calculating man and no one in the family could stand their ground against his authority.

Seeing the situation getting out of hand, Vivek's mother also jumped in and said to Vivek, "Say sorry to *dadaji* right now. I just don't understand what exactly has gone into your head. We spend Rs. 1,500 an hour to train you with the best teachers in the town, send you to the top-rated school in the country and give you facilities that many children only dream of, and this is how you behave? By speaking insolently to your elders?! This is not how we have trained you to be. Say sorry to your grandfather or else be ready to face the consequences."

Vivek had all his hopes pinned on his hero, his father. He secretly wished his father, with just one answer, would shut them all up and rescue him from the shackles of their authority. He wanted his father to take his side. But Adarsh felt helpless. On the one hand, he had to follow his father's order and, on the other, he wanted to be the father his son wanted him to be. He said, "I think your mother and *dadaji* are right, Vivek. You mustn't retort when speaking to your elders and, most importantly, you musn't go against their wishes. If *dadaji* thinks engineering would be a better option for you, then you must listen to him and do as he wishes. After all, he doesn't want to harm you. Whatever he is saying is for your good. In fact, I suggest you focus more on studying science, as you are weak at it, than on whiling away your time playing your guitar."

Vivek's dream came crashing down in that moment. The pain in his heart was there to stay. It had begun breaking into pieces even before his father had started to talk, because he knew that his father had weakened. He was no longer his idol. He was now a friend-turned-foe, someone Vivek would never be able to trust and love. And when the most important people in life fall, it creates a void within that can never be filled up.

Vivek's life and dreams were shattered. he was not interested in knowing the reason behind his father's choice, whether it was respect for his own father or the fear of being disowned from the business, because, at the end of the day, what was important was that he had let Vivek down. From that day onwards, Vivek shaped himself into a different human being. He started to remain aloof from his family and stayed shut in his room. He would while away hours doing nothing or studying science. He would avoid any conversations at the lunch and dinner. His father would try to chat with him, but he would answer every question very briefly. The cord was cut that day. Everyone could feel it. But there was no one to attempt to reconnect it.

Vivek continued to live with his family only as an obligation. Whether as a way to run from his family or to kill anything desirable inside him, he finally decided to give in and study engineering. He thought hostel life would help him find an escape and he would be better off without any of his so-called family members. All his life he was escaping things and situations and the hostel seemed like the perfect way to do so.

He was a good student to begin with and eventually turned out to be a good science student as well. He would spend hours preparing for various entrance exams. When he was in the ninth grade, as part of his well-in-advance preparation, he enrolled himself in FIITJEE classes and spent hours trying to crack the most difficult equations. Learning and practicing formulae and theories became a part of his daily life. His focus was clear and he knew he would be able to make it. His aim was to get into the best engineering institute and he worked dedicatedly to achieve that. Early on, he had instilled in himself the dream of working for the best and he was self-oriented enough to make his dream a reality. He was a topper in school and so cracking the IIT entrance was not difficult for him. He secured himself a seat in IIT Delhi. It was time to move on, away from the suffocating and frustrating atmosphere of his home. The list of achievements and the hidden pleasure of escaping family life grew when he later got accepted into IIM. His parents were very happy and extremely proud of his achievements, but they knew little about his real predicament, that he was a lost boy in need of love, a sense of security, a boy who needed to believe that there was a home for him somewhere.

The day he left for the hostel, his father had come to see him off, but Vivek was not concerned with any sentimental interactions. He felt that bidding farewell was a very mechanical thing he had to do and he did it. Beyond that, he had absolutely no bond with either of his parents. With his sister, he behaved how an elder brother should. They always maintained an unspoken distance. But then, they were taught to do so, owing to the family values they had grown up with. An occasional display of affection during festivals like *rakhi* and *bhai dooj* and on occasions like birthdays was all the relaxation they permitted themselves in each other's company. There was nothing more to their relationship. Maybe the strain that he felt due to the lack of a connection with their parents was the reason for the awkwardness between his sister and him.

Lost in his thoughts about his growing up years, he was suddenly brought back to the present as the train jerked to a halt at some station. He felt a strange and indefinable lightness. The idea of going to Pune for a brief course in meditation at the yoga institute was thrilling. Vivek was sure that it would bring about a qualitative change in his lifestyle. It was sure to flush out the toxic thoughts and memories from his mind. He had been the happiest person when the train had pulled out from New Delhi station at 1:30 in the afternoon. *A new phase in my life begins from this very instant,* he had whispered to himself. Now, as it waited at a random platform en route, all he knew was that it would resume its journey in a matter of a few minutes and he would once again start his thought journey, escaping into another world. But, as had always been the case with him, life had other plans. Nothing could have prepared him for the kinds of changes that were about to unfold in his life. Whether they were for good or for bad would depend on the extent to which he accepted them.

While he was busy fishing for thoughts, a man suddenly sat next to him. Feeling uncomfortable in yet another intruder's company, Vivek felt a sense of irritation taking over him. He wanted the new stranger to just vanish and so protested, "I think you are sitting on the wrong berth. This one is reserved in my name. Look here, I have the ticket with me. My name is printed on it."

"Never mind with your claims. Your claim over the reserved seat begins only after eight o'clock." With a grin on his face, the man started to push his luggage into the space under the berth, not bothered about Vivek's discomfort. Once done with settling his luggage, the man continued, "We are daily commuters, my friend. All officers on this route know us. We do it every day. No one can stop us here. Even the ticket checkers don't dare to ask us for tickets." He paused and grinned. "Perhaps you're travelling by this train for the first time. No wonder you don't know how things operate here. Ticket or no ticket, we can sit anywhere. If you have any problem, go talk to the T.T.E. Maybe he'll be able to put some sense in your head."

After sharing these words of wisdom, the man started to laugh.

"Just the other day, a ticket checker was adamant about checking the ticket of a daily commuter. He kept pressuring him to produce the ticket. Poor checker didn't know the man was a local goon. Every day, he travels for short distances without paying for any of the services. Bad luck! It was just not the checker's day. He didn't stop despite being told not to ask that fellow for the ticket. Suddenly, the local goon got angry and do you know what he did in his fit of anger?"

Vivek just stared at the man with bewilderment and surprise.

"The goon slapped the ticket checker twice. Once to tell him about the mistake he made and the second time to tell him who he was and that he shouldn't mess with him again. Poor ticket checker! Imagine how humiliated a man in his position must have felt at being slapped by a local goon! But what to do, this is the norm here and, if someone tries to play with the norm, he is bound to face the consequences. Trust me, my friend, no ticket checker has since tried to pester everyday commuters for tickets."

Vivek was shocked. He did not know what to say to the man. He was scared, too, of the possibility of meeting the same fate as the ticket checker if he insisted on telling this man to move to some other compartment. He wanted to bash the man up, but lacked the courage. He decided to ignore the fellow and let him share his berth.

Vivek noticed that the family sitting across him was equally shocked to hear the story that had just been narrated. The father particularly had a protective look on his face, as if to say, "Please do not harm my family—I will do as you please." Not being the kind to offer reassurance or sympathy to strangers, Vivek stayed quiet and once again began looking out the window, thinking of the kind of people that ruled the country. He thought of how small towns had become like banana republics where law and order did not act as a deterrent. Anyone with a small amount of power was "big" and could call the shots, with higher authorities coming crawling to them. He felt immense unhappiness at the way the nation was developing, losing its culture, traditions and the spirit of giving.

After a few stops, the man who was occupying Vivek's berth got off and all of them heaved a sigh of relief. It was as if they had got a heavy load off their chests. Moreover, the flowing green fields outside were soothing enough to calm his anxious nerves. The sight of the greenery made him reflect happily on the fact that at least the rural landscape was throbbing with fertility and abundance. The beautiful fields looked stunning. *The best way to enjoy the country life is through a train journey*, he thought. The vivid glimpses it offered of life in rural areas and small satellite towns were amazing. Zipping past the green fields, mud houses, little street urchins waving to passing trains, women going back home with water pitchers or grass bundles placed on their heads, cattle grazing, menfolk working in fields…it was like a kaleidoscope of the real India. This India was real because it balanced the other end of the spectrum that seemed to be progressing at the speed of light.

As a kid, Vivek had always loved train journeys. It was only when he joined the big fat corporate world that he started travelling business class on plush aircrafts and got disconnected with the India beyond shopping malls and five-star comforts. Travelling by train again today gave him a sense of joy and he felt as if he was meeting an old friend after a gap of many years. The connection he felt with this India on this particular journey was an emotional one. He once again realized the power of nature and simplicity. He was at last both happy and relieved about having embarked on this journey.

Vivek's train of thought was once again broken, this time by the husband-wife duo sitting across from him. Their animated laughter caught him by surprise and he was once again brought back to reality. They were looking at each other while the children were busy playing video games. The couple seemed to enjoy a great rapport. The woman was talkative and was excitedly and animatedly explaining something to her husband. All the while, the husband was looking admiringly into her eyes. They were quite comfortable touching each other out of affection from time to time, in a teasing and playful manner. *They are undoubtedly in love with each other*, thought Vivek, and he started to feel a hint of jealousy. Together, they reminded him of his own unhappiness. He had trained himself to run away from the very notion of love. Vivek had felt there was no such thing since as far back as he could remember. It was just a distant concept to him, nothing too fascinating. So far, he had been very practical in matters of love. Unsurprisingly, he had decided to leave his family and wife behind without the slightest regret. Of all things, love was certainly not the pull that would take him back to them again.

So now, face-to-face with this lovey-dovey couple, he just could not relate to them or understand how two people could be so in love that they only had eyes for each other. He felt that this idea of publicly displaying affection was obscene and annoying and he wanted to walk out of the compartment. But he realized it would not be such a good idea, as the people outside the compartment posed more of a threat to his need for loneliness than this family.

Here, the children were vibrant and seemingly free of any issues, but his own experience was different, and a bitter one. And he had no choice but to remain there and remember it.

Memories flashed across his mind.

His parents got along smoothly with each other, but there did not exist any real warmth between them. Everything was quite formal at home and, even though he was given the usual gentle care by them, there never really was any emotional involvement. His father was always busy with his business, while his mother was occupied with her own social work. Neither parent could make time for their son. He was looked after mainly by his maid.

Besides, his mother was a strict disciplinarian. She had never responded well to her son's own emotional gestures. One day, when Vivek's mother had been sitting and talking with her friends, Vivek had come running up to her, thrown his tiny arms around her, and cried out happily, "I love you, mom!"

Her friends had laughed.

"He's starved for your love!" one of them observed.

"Where does he study?" asked another friend.

"How beautiful is the love between a mother and her child! My children never do anything like this!" observed someone sarcastically.

"It's really hard to teach a child proper etiquette!" commented a grim-looking friend with an aquiline nose.

His mother's face had gone red. Shaking off his tender, tiny hands, she said brusquely, "Oh, what nonsense! What's this, Vivek? Don't you see I'm busy?"

Her displeasure expressing itself in her caustic tone, she turned towards the maid and said, "Rammo, you're careless in carrying out your duties! Why do you have to spoil the kid? See, you haven't even combed his hair and dressed him properly! I'm not happy about it." She stopped for a few moments, searching for the appropriate words that could get her anger across to both of them. "Vivek, you aren't acting like a good boy! Mom is very angry with you. Now, go away immediately with Rammo and do whatever you want.

Come to your mom only when you're asked to." She paused, and then, fixing her gaze upon Vivek, she asked, "Do you understand what I am trying to drill into your head?"

Vivek was confounded by his mother's strange reaction. However, he simply said, teary-eyed, "Yes, Mom! I get it. I'm sorry! I'll never come to you again, unless asked by you."

"Good!" said his mother with pride. "Nice boy! Mom's darling!" She paused and flashed a smile at her friends. Then, raising her voice, she said, "Now, go away from here!"

He had gone away. His mother's rejection of his innocent overture left an indelible scar on his mind.

"My mom doesn't love me!" he told Rammo.

"Why do you say that? All mothers love their children," said Rammo to console him.

"Then why did she scold me like that?" Vivek asked, sounding despondent.

"Perhaps she didn't like the way you were dressed," said Rammo. All of a sudden, he leaned back and rested his head on Rammo's bosom. Gently, she passed her hand over him.

"Will you be my mom?" he suddenly asked Rammo.

Initially, she was shocked and disturbed. All she managed to say, with great difficulty, was, "Yes, I'll be your mom." She did not say anything more for a long time. Then, she whispered, her voice quivering with emotion, "I'm your mom!"

Vivek's face brightened up. He kissed her forehead gently and said emotionally, "Mom, I'm very happy!"

At night, he would cling to her assuring body. The warmth and odor of her body would soothe him. It was like a healing ointment. She would tell him ancient, mythological stories about brave and ideal kids, stories that had always been part of the social and cultural life of the people of India. Then, one day, he addressed Rammo as "mom" before his own mother. And that was the end of it.

"What's this, Rammo?" she had asked the maid.

"I can't stop him from addressing me in that way. It's his choice. He's my young master, I can't stop him," Rammo said, trying to explain the whole thing.

"I can't accept such gross impertinence in this household," said Vivek's mom with asperity. "You can't be allowed to work here anymore. My kid is getting spoilt in your company. You must leave!"

His mother had a heart of granite. She did not pay any heed to Rammo's pleas for another chance; Rammo was sent packing unceremoniously.

Things were pretty bleak in other parts of the household, too.

Vivek's father also had an office at home. Sometimes, he would peep into his father's office, unnoticed by anyone. One day, his father caught him there.

"What are you doing here, Vivek?" he asked, looking curious.

"Dad, I want to tell you something!"

"What is it?"

"Our school is putting up a play tomorrow!"

"So, what about it?"

"I'm playing the main part in it!"

"Really? I'm very proud of you."

"Won't you come to see it?"

"I can't."

"Why not?"

"I've a very important meeting tomorrow. Ask your mom."

"She is going for some protest rally somewhere."

"Well, tough luck, son," said his father, dismissing his request.

When he had grown up a little more, Vivek had learned to put up with the modalities of their big household. However, it destroyed the tender feelings in him. He now responded to everything rationally, just like his parents had demonstrated to him at all times. He had obviously had no idea how his parents' apathy in bringing up their child was going to affect his emotional and personal life later.

He came back to the present. The husband and his wife were laughing loudly at something. The children were laughing, too. In order to distract himself from the couple, he took out a book from his handbag: *The Economic Way of Thinking* by Paul Heyne. Despite being an engineering student, Vivek had a keen interest in economics. Maybe it had to do with his genes, belonging as he did to a business family; he had always kept himself up to date with what was happening in the world of economics. When he decided to leave his house, books on economics were among the few things that made their way into his suitcase. He felt that they would help provide him comfort during long boring moments of loneliness. A decision well-made, he thought to himself when he found himself stuck in a train compartment with a bunch of unwanted people. He tried to concentrate on the book, but the constant chatter of the couple and their children kept on disturbing him.

"Do not try to cheat."

"I am not cheating. It is you who is trying to cheat."

"I saw you deliberately throwing the dice in such a way that the number totaled."

"Shut up. I did not. You are a fool and a loser and so always behave like a crybaby whenever you see yourself losing."

"You are a liar."

"No, you are."

The children and their constant banter had started to get on his nerves. Finally, tired of trying to make sense of what he was reading, he closed the book and put it away.

As he reached for his suitcase with the book, he felt as if someone was watching him. He looked up and met the eyes of the woman's husband. They were following his every moment with the scrutiny of a security officer. Vivek felt uncomfortable for a brief moment. In order to avoid being rude to his fellow passenger, he passed him a smile and again started to look outside the window. But, from the corner of his eye, Vivek could see that the husband was still staring at him. Though the man had plain looks, his piercing eyes were beautiful and added a sense of charisma to his gaze and yet, at the same time, something about them was making Vivek uneasy. He felt as if the man had read his mind and the entire story of his life in a flash. Disturbed at the prospect of a total stranger understanding him at such a deep level without actually knowing anything, Vivek became increasingly uncomfortable.

While Vivek was desperately thinking of ways to escape the man's gaze, the man asked him, in a soft voice, "Where are you heading, *babuji*? Divi?"

Vivek shot a look of confusion at the man, as if trying to figure out whether to answer him or not.

"By the way, I am Paresh Kashyap. This is my wife, Neelu, and these are my children, Pooja and Rajesh. Say hello to uncle, children!"

Before Vivek could decide whether to speak with him or not, the man had introduced his entire clan. Vivek was left with no choice now but to introduce himself and pass the mandatory smile to his entire family, which he mechanically did.

He did tell Paresh his name but conveniently escaped the question of where exactly he was heading. He did not want to give the impression of being a drifter to his newly introduced neighbor and his family, so he decided to keep mum.

Paresh was quite taken aback by this behavior. Getting the sense that he was intruding into Vivek's private space, he apologetically said, "I'm sorry if you felt I was trying to get a bit too friendly by asking about your destination, but believe me, I had no intention of interfering. I asked it instinctively. So, please excuse me."

Realizing that he might also have unintentionally hurt Paresh's sentiments by being rude to him, Vivek quickly changed his expression and, in a softer tone, replied, "Oh no, please don't get me wrong. It's just that I don't open up to strangers that easily. So, I found your question a bit intrusive. I didn't mean to sound rude to you or your family, but it's just that I don't speak very often to people of your kind."

Anyone else in Paresh's place would have felt hurt and angry at Vivek's unceremonious remarks regarding his status, but Paresh was a man of pride and resilience. He knew he belonged to the lower middle stratum of the society and was no match socially for a person as well-dressed and educated as Vivek; yet, he was proud of being a self-made man. He had been ridiculed in the past, too, but had not let criticism of his social stature bog him down. He had taken strength from those criticisms and attained for himself the title of a self-made businessman who was a manufacturer of *samosas*. In Divi and one station beyond it, his *samosas* were famous and went by the name "Matru ka *samosa*," a name he himself had devised in memory of his great-grandfather. Although his business was still at a low scale, he was happy about the fact that it gave him a sense of being independent and provided for the everyday needs of his family. He knew Vivek's comments were deliberate but he ignored them and continued undaunted.

"It's okay, *babuji*. An educated man of your kind always feels wary of talking to people like us. But trust me, there is nothing to worry about. You came across as a person who is confused about something in life and desperately seeking answers to certain questions, so I thought if I could be of any help I should offer you my advice."

Vivek felt quite taken aback by Paresh's frankness. *Here is a complete stranger offering to help me, even though he does not even know I am going through! He can go on thinking of himself as some guru, but his advice is not something I am looking for at this point in time.* Agitated by Paresh's frankness, Vivek said, "Do you even know who I am? We have barely been introduced to each other and you think you have gauged my entire life and are ready with life-changing solutions? Listen, whatever your name is, I don't need your advice on anything. So please just let me be and get back to enjoying your time with your wife."

"I'm a very ordinary and simple family man. Maybe I cannot offer you solutions to your problems, as you said, but at times, talking to complete strangers helps. You know, with strangers, the advantage is that you can choose to never meet them again in life. They listen to your story. Offer their insights. And, if you don't like their advice, you can choose to ignore them and move on in life. With friends and family, that is something you can never do because you are always at the risk of upsetting them and revealing a bit too much about your innermost thoughts."

The man is pretty wise despite his humble bearings, thought Vivek. Paresh's frankness worked as an ice-breaker between them. Intrigued by his wisdom and philosophical insights, Vivek, too, warmed up to him.

"So, Paresh, right? You think if I speak my heart out to you, I'll feel better and be able to find answers to my problems?"

"Absolutely. It is not a very difficult thing I'm asking you to do. I'm my town's favorite agony aunt. Anytime someone has a problem, they come and share it with me because they know I'll always listen to them. Even my own wife at times talks nineteen to the dozen, knowing I won't interrupt her or cut her short."

Innocent, thought Vivek, but he was in no mood to discuss his life with a stranger yet. "So, what do you do, Paresh, apart from solving problems in the lives of strangers like me?"

"Oh no, you're embarrassing me now. I'm just a humble *samosa* maker. I have a small shop in Divi and from there I also supply *samosas* to railway station vendors, a few minutes away from Divi. That is how I take care of my family."

"I didn't know I was sitting in the company of a *samosa* entrepreneur," Vivek said cheekily.

"*Arre, babuji*, you are again embarrassing me with your kind words. I'm just a small businessman. I don't have a big setup either. Just one small shop from where I operate. My wife and my sister help me with my business. So it's with their support that I'm able to run the day-to-day operations. Otherwise, I don't think I have it in me to compete with the bigger players in the game. But, whatever I have right now, I'm content with it and hope it continues."

The humbleness and simplicity with which Paresh described his life struck a chord with Vivek. Since it was none of his business, he did not bother to ask Paresh anything more about his life, but he was impressed. After this mini-interaction, there was a long silence between the two. The children were playing ludo and video games and the wife had her head buried in a Hindi women's magazine that she seemed to be enjoying a lot.

After a brief period, Paresh started the conversation again, "*Babuji*, you didn't tell me where exactly you were heading?"

Worried that his uninformed state of mind would give Paresh the impression that he was a wanderer, Vivek quickly answered, without thinking, "Belgaum."

"I'm afraid you have boarded the wrong train, then—this train does not go to Belgaum. How come no one told you that? And why did you board this train without checking its name?" Paresh's anxiety at the discovery that Vivek had unknowingly boarded the wrong train was an expression of his innocent desire to help a stranger as well as his surprise that the stranger seemed clueless about where exactly he was heading. "I think you should get off at the very next station and ask the station master to help you get back to Delhi or suggest some other train."

In no mood to take any more suggestions or interference from Paresh, Vivek got irritated and said angrily, "I know this train doesn't go to Belgaum and, if it was required, I would have got off at the next station without seeking any advice from you. So please leave me alone with my thoughts for some time and spare me your 'agony aunt' advice. I request you to stop interfering in my life!"

"But, *babuji*, you said you were heading for Belgaum so I thought, since this is not the train that goes there, I'll help you deboard!" Paresh looked at his wife and children for affirmation, which they provided by nodding their heads.

Suddenly embarrassed at being caught lying, Vivek's anger subsided. "I'm sorry I lied. I'm not going to Belgaum. I deliberately boarded the train without knowing where exactly it was heading. I thought I'd get off at the last station and then see where to go from there. I did not mean to cause you so much anxiety. In fact, I'm going to Pune."

Still confused about why Vivek would lie to him about his destination, Paresh said, "Oh! I thought you'd made a mistake. I believe you are running from something—I don't see any other reason for your being on such a journey. I could tell at first sight that you were confused about something in life and had a lot going on in your head. But since I noticed you were in a pensive mood, I decided not to disturb you. So, in a way, I was correct."

Vivek knew there was no going back from this conversation. He could ask Paresh to keep quiet and mind his own business, or he could leave the compartment. However, he decided to continue chatting with Paresh. Something about Paresh made Vivek feel relaxed in his company. He felt as if he was speaking with an old friend, as if he could be himself with Paresh and not bother about Paresh's opinion of him. Paresh's pleasing personality was a big draw for Vivek. Feeling assured and happy, Vivek finally decided to speak candidly.

"To tell you the truth, yes, you are right about me. There are certain things I'm trying to escape from right now. Where to, I don't know. How, I'm completely clueless. But one thing is for sure—I want to leave my past behind and begin afresh."

"Everyone faces ups and downs in their lives. But running away from problems is not the solution. Embracing them and accepting them as challenges so that one can rebound from bad times with one's head held high is how they should be tackled," said Paresh.

"Easier said than done! Preaching this stuff is one thing, but when it comes to applying these principles in real life, we all fail," said Vivek. "What I'm trying to say is that what might appear to be a case of a simple problem-and-solution game to you might actually be a thing that is silently destroying somebody else's life. No one has the solutions to another person's problems, because the solution that might work for you in your particular situation may not have that effect in another person's life."

"Correct!" Paresh shot back. "But only when we fail are we able to rise to future occasions. I've always believed that failure is the best teacher in life. It teaches you to appreciate wins and aim better the next time. It also teaches you the worth of those who continue to stand by you in lean times and filter fair weather friends out of your life. And, yes, every person's situation might not be the same, but being positive and keeping an open mind is the key to solving all problems. That much is universally acknowledged. I'm sure you cannot possibly deny this truth."

This man has so much wisdom in him that it is hard to believe he is so modestly educated and comes from a different world altogether, thought Vivek. Maybe that was the secret of his happiness—the reason he was so sorted. Maybe his native wisdom made his everyday life better, something that many who searched incessantly failed to find.

"I agree with you," Vivek said with genuine appreciation.

By the time they were halfway through the conversation, Vivek could feel a change being wrought in him. He realized he was smiling and sometimes even laughing while exchanging and sharing thoughts with Paresh. He found the interaction stimulating and interesting, something he had not felt for ages. This perhaps was the reason he was smiling.

Noticing this, Paresh asked, "What makes you smile? I hope you don't find me laughable. I know the idea of such words coming out of my mouth may seem funny to you, but, *babuji*, I have met and dealt with many different kinds of people, so I consider myself quite experienced in human psychology. I might not have studied beyond higher secondary, but no book teaches you about life the way life teaches you about itself."

Vivek replied, "Nothing of that sort. I'm just amused at having discovered a great philosopher and businessman in the unlikeliest of places and under such strange circumstances." He did not yet want to share his innermost thoughts and feelings with Paresh, preferring to maintain the distance that was still there between them. Nevertheless, he did find him an interesting person to spend time with.

Over the next few hours, the two of them came closer and exchanged views on various subjects, covering work, family, education, children and more. Vivek slowly and eventually began to understand more about Paresh and learned that, despite coming from a very modest background, he had figured out how to be content and positive—unlike Vivek, who had had all the money and the best education and a cushy life from the very start, yet was deprived of the most basic emotional need, the need for love and belongingness, all through. All he craved was a touch of affection. All he expected from his own parents and family was that they would understand his angst. Maybe, in Paresh, he was slowly discovering a friend who would at least listen to his innermost feelings, even if he couldn't provide a solution to every problem. Vivek was now happy about having opened up to and attempted a real conversation with Paresh. *Maybe a one-on-one dialogue with all those I have ever cared for in my life has been the solution all along*, he thought. But he was also aware that this lovely conversation would soon end, as the time would come for Paresh and his family to get off the train. Vivek was now getting agitated at this prospect and also about not knowing where he would end up.

Just to take his mind off the thought of the conversation coming to an end, he decided to dive deeper into Paresh's life and understand where exactly he had gotten all his wisdom from. Since Vivek had no particular agenda in mind, knowing more about Paresh and his background would keep him intrigued for a few days.

"If you don't mind, can I ask you something?" he said.

Even though Vivek's tone still had that aristocratic quality which people usually acquire when talking to someone lower in status to them, it was not intentional.

"Of course! Ask me whatever you feel like. Although I'm not sure I can offer you any interesting answers, I shall consider myself lucky if I can be of any help to you."

"No, I'm not seeking any help from you. I just want to know a bit more about your background—where you come from and how you started this little business empire of yours."

"*Babuji*, I'm a man of very humble origins. My great-grandfather had migrated to the small town of Divi decades ago and that is where all the generations of my family have lived ever since. His farming and agricultural background did not help him much. His own brother fleeced him of all his property. He became a daily wage laborer in order to support his family. Since we were poor and my grandfather didn't have the means to support my father's education, he remained an uneducated man. But my father was a determined person who felt that education was required for the next generation to prosper. So, when my parents had me, they sent me to a government school nearby. But because of the scarcity of work and my father's declining health, money became a problem. I had to drop out of school at an early stage. I went to school until Class 12 and that is how I can read and write in Hindi. I do understand English, too, but it is not my language and I have no command over it. I'm quite fluent in Hindi and Gujarati, but I've never been confident about the English language."

Vivek listened to Paresh's story with fascination, but also reminded himself that it was a typical story of a poor Indian. There was nothing new about it. He felt pained at the fact that, even though the country had progressed at breakneck speed in certain respects, there were still families like Paresh's that continued to live in poverty. Even when governments made education free for children from backward classes, there remained many who went without even the most basic education. The country was touching the sky in terms of the progress its scientists and engineers were making in various fields, but, at the same time, there was a section of society that had never even enjoyed the luxury of being a student.

Sad at the state of affairs in the country, Vivek felt compelled to ask Paresh, "So, how did this *samosa* business of yours come into being? Your health and physical appearance don't seem to suggest that you are much of a foodie. So how did you get into making *samosas*?"

"I was very young when my father died, only around 14–15, I believe. My sister and my mother had to be looked after, so I decided to help my mother bring home the bacon. We were in such dire straits that, on bitter cold nights, my mother, my sister and I used to share one thin blanket that my mother had found lying in some bin. It was tattered when she found it. She sewed it together so that it could provide us some comfort at night. We never had enough clothes to flaunt. I possessed just two pairs of shirts and two pairs of trousers. My sister wore used clothes given to my mother by her employers.

"My mother, *babuji*, was a fighter of sorts. She worked nights as a nanny in people's homes. She was a great cook. She earned money through that skill of hers, while cooking food for the affluent families in Ankleshwar. She never let us see her pain or stress. She was a really loving mother in every sense. Those were really hard days, but all through it, we remained one unit and that helped us sail through the harsh times. It was basically her love for cooking that she imparted to me early in life. She had learned to make delicious *samosas* from my grandfather, who himself was an excellent chef. It's his recipe that has been passed down to me and I have been able to make something out of it. My shop's name, 'Matru ka Samosa,' is a tribute to him. He used to call me Matru when I was a little boy.

"Because I wasn't well-educated, I couldn't have gone to a bigger city and found a job for myself. So I decided to stay and do something in my own town. Besides, if everyone rushes to the bigger cities and becomes obsessed with developing those cement jungles, who is going to think about smaller towns like ours? Of all the things in the world, the one thing I was confident of being perfect at was making *samosas*, so I borrowed a few hundred rupees from a couple of my friends, bought a cook-top, a few utensils and the required amount of raw material, and got started.

"I was only 16 at that time and still a novice, but with the support of my mother and little sister, I was soon able to expand and grow beyond the town. The journey has been full of challenges but I have thoroughly enjoyed it. There have been times when I could not meet the demands for huge orders as the vendor would refuse to give me an advance and I didn't have enough money to buy material on my own, or because climatic conditions caused my *samosas* to become soggy, or because I was not able to send my delivery on time due to some problem, yet I knew that I'd be able to overcome these problems and start all over again the next day. I have seen terrible lows and somewhat normal highs in my business, but I feel content with the way it has turned out. I am grateful to my family, for it is with their love and support that I have been able to rise every time I fell."

Vivek was tempted to ask him about the source of his calm resilience and he eventually did ask.

"I don't think there is any one particular reason for it," said Paresh. "In fact, I didn't think of myself as a tough person until you mentioned it, but, for me, the fact that I'm a man who comes from nowhere and is struggling hard to make a name for himself and provide comfort to his family is enough to keep me motivated. Had it not been for them, I wouldn't have dared to do anything like this."

How lucky this man is, thought Vivek. *His family is there to help him bloom and so, today, despite not having much, he stays positive and content.* At that point, he wished he hadn't asked Paresh about his story, as he could feel a hint of jealousy overtaking him. He knew he was talking to a man who was nothing in comparison to himself, yet, in many ways, that man had exceeded him in life and in love.

Paresh noticed the lost look on Vivek's face and stopped himself from speaking any further.

"Are you okay, *babuji*? You seem to be worried about something."

"No, no, I'm fine, Paresh. It's just that I found your story very interesting." Vivek did not want to use the words "touching" or "inspiring" to describe Paresh's story, because he feared it would give Paresh a reason for self-pride and that was the last thing he wanted.

"Enough of me chattering about my past," Paresh said. "*Babuji*, now that you have heard so much about me, why don't we talk about you?"

Fearing he would have to say his part, Vivek tried to dodge the question and, with a shake of his head, said, "There is nothing in my life worth mentioning. I have not lived through as many highs and lows as you. It would be better if we left it at that."

Understanding that it was not the right time to coax the story out of him, Paresh decided to let Vivek be, but still offered him consoling words. "I know you seem to be disturbed about something. I'm sure something terrible must have happened to you in the past that you are bitter about, and I don't want to interfere in your personal matters. Still, can I say something?"

"Paresh, no philosophical words can offer me any solace right now," said Vivek.

"I'm going to say a very practical thing to you and I hope you won't mind. Considering you aren't too sure where exactly you are heading, and since you don't seem to have much of an agenda currently and are not in a rush of any sort either, why don't you come and stay with me in my house in Divi for a few days? It'll be a good change for you and, whenever you are sure of where you want to go, you can leave," said Paresh.

Taken aback by this sudden offer, Vivek didn't know how to react. He had not expected to be offered free advice and then a place to live by a complete stranger. A stranger whom at first he had found to be irritating and later thought of as interesting; however, he was not very comfortable with the idea of sharing a house with someone he had just met and knew nothing about (except that he was a *samosa* maker). Slowly regaining his senses and, still recovering from the shock of being offered a place to stay, Vivek thought of a reply. He said in a polite tone, "Thank you very much, Paresh, for your kindness and the offer, but I don't think I can really accept it. Don't get me wrong, but I think I am okay and will figure out soon what to do next. But I'm touched by your thoughtfulness and really feel humbled by your gesture."

"I'm sorry if something I said offended you, but I thought that, since you have nothing particular in mind, I could help you by offering you a place to stay for a couple of days."

"No, not at all, Paresh. I'm not hurt or anything. In fact, I think it was really considerate of you, but I really don't wish to be a burden on you or your family. I think having a stranger around in the house can be a bit of a nuisance for anyone and I really don't want to be the cause of any discomfort, especially now that you have been so kind to me."

"You are again embarrassing me. Trust me, neither my wife nor my kids will feel awkward about your staying with us. My wife is always very happy to have guests over, as it allows us to socialize and meet and talk to people, which we usually do not get to do in our small town. And my kids will also be happy to have you around." said Paresh.

"But I can't, Paresh. I barely know you and vice-versa. I don't think it'd be a good arrangement for either of us," Vivek said, shrugging his shoulders.

On that, Paresh's wife said, cutting in, "*Namaste, babuji!*" Vivek turned to her. She had an inherent dignity and smartness about her. She continued, "I'm Neelu Kashyap. Please accept my husband's offer."

Vivek was moved by her warmth. After brooding over the situation for a while, he said, "Right now, I'm at sixes and sevens. It's so sudden!"

A smile came to Neelu's face. Fixing her gaze upon Vivek, she said, "We'd be honored by your presence in our household. We treat guests as our own family members."

Vivek found her simplicity and straightforwardness very striking. Not saying anything immediately, he silently considered the pros and cons of the offer. Both Paresh and Neelu kept looking at him imploringly. At last, breaking a long silence, Vivek said, "I wish you and your family all the happiness. But, right now, I don't think that I should accept your invitation."

"Why not?" asked Neelu.

"I hate the very idea of being a liability to someone," said Vivek.

"A guest isn't a liability in our culture," said Neelu, protesting.

Paresh said, "Please, *babuji*! Don't think like that. You're not going to be a burden on us in any way. You can help my kids with their studies and daily homework and also teach them about other things. You can also help me with my work if you feel like. You won't be made to feel like a person wasting his time. Trust me. We will all be delighted to have you."

By now, Paresh's wife was also smiling and looking at Vivek as if expecting him to consent. Since he did not have anything to look forward to and had promised himself before embarking on this journey that he would go with the flow, Vivek thought that perhaps this was how his life was to take shape and decided finally to accept the invitation. Thrilled to have a new guest at home, the entire family was overcome by joy. But, still doubtful about whether he had made the correct move and whether he would actually be able to adjust to this new lifestyle, Vivek sat silently in a daze, waiting for the train to reach Divi.

A New Home

It was in the wee hours of morning that the train came to a halt. Vivek woke up to the sudden shock of someone shaking his shoulders frantically. It felt as if the train had met with an accident and he was being tossed around in his compartment.

He responded with a startled, "What happened?!"

Realizing that his shaking had frightened Vivek, Paresh said, "I'm sorry for suddenly waking you up, but we have reached Divi. It's time for all of us to leave."

Vivek wasn't used to being treated with such familiarity and considered it undesirable and uncouth. For a moment, he wanted to rethink his decision to accept Paresh's offer, but he realized it was too late and he did not want to offend Paresh and his family. Getting back to his senses and on to his feet, Vivek pulled out the tiny suitcase from under the berth he was occupying, slung his handbag over his shoulder, and followed Paresh and his family towards the exit. Reluctantly, he looked around the station and, one last time, asked himself if he was making the right move.

"Come on, *babuji*. Give me your suitcase and I'll help you get off."

He disembarked thinking about how he was plunging into a new life, a life of unknown journeys and destinations. Together, all of them proceeded towards the main exit of the station. It was not a small station. There were newspaper and magazine sellers on the platform, and a major portion of the space was occupied by a food stall whose sign read "Matru ka Samosa." This was a pleasant surprise for Vivek.

A few passengers were asleep on the platform as well, perhaps waiting for their respective trains to arrive. Because it was still very early in the day, the station was relatively quiet. Vivek checked his watch to see that it was only 4:45 a.m. He followed Paresh up and down multiple flights of steps. After a few minutes, they reached an auto stand and took two autos. Paresh sat with his wife in one while Vivek shared space with Paresh's two children in the other. After a bone-shattering journey of 20 minutes, the auto stopped outside a small independent house.

After much haggling with the two *autowalas*, Paresh paid them Rs 30 each and turned towards Vivek.

"These *autowalas*! They always do this. They agree to one price at the beginning of the journey and, when you get off, their prices suddenly shoot up. I know you must not be used to travelling in autos and haggling with them, but I am a master at it."

So he is shrewd with money, too, thought Vivek.

It was only when Paresh pointed towards his house that Vivek properly took it in. A double-story bungalow, painted in tones of crème and pink, it had a huge verandah and in one corner of the yard was a small garden-like area with flowers blooming and a thatched roof to protect it from the harsh sun. When Vivek entered through the gate, he noticed a small cement structure in another corner of the property that had a *tulsi* plant jutting out of it. He realized

Neelu must have gotten the structure erected there, as was common among typical Indian housewives.

At first glance, Vivek was rather pleased with the house. It appeared tidy, cozy and comfortable. The interiors were modest. Although there was nothing striking about the way the house had been designed or decorated, it exuded a sense of homeliness. He knew that he would not find here any of the comforts he had grown up and lived with until yesterday, but he didn't want those comforts either. He was happy to be "home" at last.

Having instructed his son to carry Vivek's luggage, Paresh said, "Come, I'll show you to your room."

The three of them proceeded upstairs. At the end of a corridor was a small yet spacious room that was going to be Vivek's for as long as he wished to stay with the family. When Paresh opened the door to the room, Vivek was happy to see a huge window that overlooked the green fields outside. He immediately liked the room and told Paresh that it was just perfect for him.

"I know, *babuji*, the house and the rooms are a bit small for you. This is all I can offer you at the moment, but, believe me, you'll start loving the place once you become acquainted with it. My room is downstairs. Rajesh's room is right next to yours, so, in case you want anything, you can call out to him or me anytime you wish. He is a very efficient boy and knows every nook and corner of this town and what to get from where."

Looking at his son, he said, "Look, Rajesh, *babuji* is new in town, so he'll require your assistance. Make sure you are available to him. If I get to hear a single complaint about you, you know what I'm capable of doing."

Vivek sensed a mix of both adoration and slight strictness in Paresh's voice while he spoke to his son. He realized that Paresh was not just a doting father; he knew how to discipline his kids. Another facet of this man. Vivek's admiration for him grew one notch.

Turning back to Vivek, Paresh said, "It's a bit early for me to take you around town and I know you must be tired of all the travelling. So make yourself comfortable and sleep for a few hours now. I'll see you in some time."

"Yeah, perfectly fine," replied Vivek.

Paresh turning his back to Vivek and made his way out of the room, but was called back in by Vivek.

"Ji, *babuji*, tell me. Do you want anything?"

Before Vivek could answer, he told his son to rush downstairs and fetch water for Vivek.

"I'm sorry. In this haste of showing you your room, I forgot to offer you water or tea."

"Oh, no, Paresh, please don't bother with such formalities. I'm absolutely fine. It's just that I wanted to say—" He paused to find the correct words. After a long, awkward silence, Vivek continued, "Thank you! You don't, perhaps, realize the amount of good you have done to me by providing me a place in your home. I mean…I know I started out without an agenda and probably wouldn't have come to this town and stayed with a strange family, but something inside me convinced me that you are a good man. You're perhaps a person I can trust. It was after talking to you in the train that

I felt as if a burden was being lifted off my heart and your conduct was primarily responsible for my decision to come to this place. So, thank you, is all I wanted to say."

Vivek's appreciation made Paresh very happy. With an emotional look on his face, he said, "Please don't say all these things to me. I didn't do it to make you feel inferior or anything. I did it because I felt that, if my help, at any level, could help you find a way back to where you started, then I should go ahead and extend a caring hand to you. I know you might think that I am a stupid fellow, you know, the kind who goes about offering unsolicited help to strangers, but, *babuji*, that is not the case. I go out of my way to offer whatever help I can to anyone in dire need of it. It gives me immense joy and pleasure in return and makes me feel that my life's purpose has been served. So, if there is anybody to thank here, then it is you, for accepting the offer of a small man like me."

"You are no small or ordinary man, Paresh. You are gifted and perhaps you aren't aware of it. But we shall reserve this conversation for some other day. I'm tired now. I'll meet you downstairs in a couple of hours. And, yes, once again, thank you!"

***

When Vivek woke up, he realized he uninterruptedly slept for almost five hours, something he had not managed to do for years. Since his father's death and the end of his hostel life, Vivek had lived with a disturbed mind. There was so much going on in his head all the time that sleep would just not come. He had turned into an insomniac. After many sessions with psychiatrists and different kinds of therapy, he had come to the conclusion that this was how his life was going to be. Deprived of love first, then deprived of sleep. Since he had no will to fight his own demons, he had decided to surrender himself to them and learned to adjust to this problem. But today was a different day, almost like a new beginning. He was already feeling good about it. The languor was gone—he was fresh as a lily. Soaking in the sun and taking in the smell of a town whose existence he had been unaware of was sitting well with him and he was feeling joyous. He went downstairs to find the house almost empty. It was noon and he was hungry, but he did not call out for Rajesh as he felt that would be asking a bit too much from his benefactors. He decided to go out on his own and fetch himself some local cuisine wherever he could find it.

Wandering through the lanes of the area, he soon realized that Divi was not what he had thought it was. It was not a village and certainly not an undeveloped town. There were houses of all kinds: big, small, *haveli*-like, occupied by people of various backgrounds. It had a mix of educated and uneducated crowds; he could make that out from the way the people were dressed. There were cars on the streets, and every 500 meters, there were shops selling utilities, electronics and other things. He spotted a Maruti Suzuki showroom and was happy to know that even satellite towns like these were receptive to change and had aspirations of being in the same league as the metros and cosmopolitan cities of India.

He had often thought that there were many opportunities bustling in the by-lanes of such towns. All that people needed was guidance, and they could be well-settled for life. Lost in these thoughts, he suddenly stumbled upon a small snack shop. The prospect of eating hot straight-from-the-wok *kachoris* and *jalebis* with a cup of tea tempted him to try the place out. He ordered two *kachoris* and a cup of tea. Gulping down the yummy tea with the equally delicious snack, he tried to remember when he'd last enjoyed such a simple yet satisfying meal.

Until he reached the shop, he had not realized how hungry he was. But the fragrance of the food was such that it evoked hunger pangs in him and he was happy that the decision to eat at that vendor had not turned out to be a regrettable one. Although Vivek's stomach was on the verge of bursting thanks to the overdose of *kachoris* and tea, he was still tempted to round off his breakfast with a *jalebi*. He requested one and was satisfied.

Life in towns like Divi was all about finding happiness in the small things, like a cup of tea or a plate of scrumptious snacks. Back in Vivek's hometown, the pace of life did not allow its residents to get a breather. People worked here, too, but also knew how to enjoy life. If food could give so much happiness and satisfaction, it was intriguing to imagine what other things could do.

He decided to get *jalebis* packed for Paresh's family. He had the shopkeeper pack half a kilo and started making his way home. He had wandered the streets of Divi for a good two hours, trying to familiarize himself with his new address. He thought life there would be a lot simpler if he knew exactly where to find what and whom to approach when in need.

He spotted a phone booth and decided to call his mother as part of his routine and to inquire about her health. Vivek's steadfast mother had become a kind of a recluse after his father's death. Although she had been a fiery and forthright social activist once, anyone who met her now would find it hard to believe that. His father's death had been quite a shock for her and she had slowly given up all worldly things to retire into a life of aloofness and solitude. She now preferred to spend more time in their family retreat in Shimla or at her daughter's home in the U.S. That provided her with all the privacy she now loved. She had very few friends whom she was in touch with and Neha, the older of her two children, was her only confidante. But it was not always a hunky-dory relationship between those two. There were occasions when they did not see eye-to-eye.

Vivek's older sister, Neha, had inherited their mother's independent streak but was much like their father in matters of social skills. She was manipulative in her dealings with others and knew how to have her own way with them. This characteristic of hers had always been a matter of discord between mother and daughter. But once Neha had passed the stage of teenage angst and her mother had mellowed down owing to her acceptance of the fact that Neha's rebelliousness was an intrinsic part of her nature, the two made peace with each other. There also came a stage when they gave each other all the space they needed. So, when the mother discovered her daughter was meeting boys and going out with them, she did not lose sleep over it. She knew trying to control the situation would only make matters worse for both of them. She decided to let Neha be.

When Neha finally announced to her parents that she was in love with an office colleague of hers and would like to marry him, they did not make a huge fuss. They went to meet the boy and his family and, within a matter of two weeks, a day for the marriage was fixed. They decided to do it quickly, as the boy was to go to the U.S. in a couple of weeks and would stay there until the end of his project.

Memories flashed across Vivek's mind. He was in the second year of his engineering course when he was informed over the phone of his sister's marriage. He took five days' leave from college and came home to much revelry. That was perhaps the only time he remembered seeing the entire family together. Everyone was happy and emotional, because Neha would soon go away to a completely strange land. But it all took place with much fanfare and, the day after the wedding, Vivek left for his hostel. Staying back in that house did not make sense to him; he found all the revelry and the great show of affection an unnecessary, dream-like sideshow that was soon going to end. He wanted to be gone before it culminated in a nightmare. So, after bidding the customary goodbyes to his father, mother and uncle and aunt, he returned to his hostel life.

It was also the last time he saw his father alive.

A few months later, he received another call from home, this time to inform him that his father had suffered a massive heart attack and had been admitted to an I.C.U. His mother had made attempts to reconcile him with his father previously, but all in vain. She had called a few days back to tell him that father was unwell and wanted to see him.

"*Haan*, Ma, tell me, how are you?"

"How can I be fine seeing your father in this condition?"

"What happened to him?"

"He is not well, Vivek. But he will neither admit that he is sick nor change his ways. Please come home and see him and try to put some sense in his head."

"Can you tell me in clear words what is wrong with him?"

"A few days ago, he complained of some uneasiness in his heart and so we immediately took him to a hospital. The doctors admitted him and now they say there are some complications in his lungs because of which they will have to keep him there for some tests."

"You should have told me about this before."

"I tried, but he said he did not want to disturb you. He does not want your studies to get affected."

"By not telling me anything, all you are achieving is your purpose of making me realize that I am not required by you."

"Please, Vivek, not this time. I really am worried for your father's health. Do try and understand the situation. We both love you and wish you could see and feel that, too."

"Yeah, Ma, you are right. You guys do love me a lot!"

"Stop being sarcastic, Vivek."

"Okay. Can I speak with him on the phone?"

"He is in the I.C.U. Phones are not allowed inside."

"I will try and come as soon as possible to see him."

"Please try and come by tomorrow. He really wants to meet you. He said he wants to see you and talk to you one last time before anything serious happens to him."

"Stop being foolish, Ma. Nothing will happen. I have an exam the day after, so I will leave after that."

"I will wait for you."

"Do keep me posted about his health and, if you need something, let me know."

"I just want you here. That's all I need from you."

"Okay. Bye. I will talk to you later." Hanging up, Vivek suddenly felt a vacant space within him. This feeling intensified further when he received a phone call from his sister, Neha, at midnight.

"Vivek, you must come home, even if it is only for one day," Neha told Vivek anxiously.

Voice even and somewhat cold, Vivek said, "I've very, very important classes to attend, my dear *didi*. My third semester exams are around the corner. They're the ones that'll contribute to my becoming an engineer."

Sensing his indifference, she said, "Don't give me that! You want to take revenge on the old guy, don't you?"

Vivek laughed and then said rather unpleasantly, "We cannot escape the consequences of our actions."

Incensed, Neha replied, "How can you have such an unfeeling heart!"

"Neha, listen to me attentively," said Vivek in a low but firm voice. "We belong to a time in which being a sentimental person means hurting yourself. My dear sis, relationships and tender emotions are worth shit in this world of boundaries and territories. Our parents are the perfect embodiments of feelinglessness. Yes, all through their lives, they have been busy pursuing their own ambitions. Now, today, their sham of a life seems to be falling apart! What can I do about it?"

Hearing his angry and bitter words, all Neha could say was, "This is the time to be generous!"

"Really, my sweet sis?"

"You seem to have been dehydrated of all human emotions!"

"Love and respect aren't one-way roads," he said, fuming.

"His flesh has melted away. The very sight of him… it's scary. Like a worm, he keeps rolling over in his bed. Occasionally, he mumbles your name, and, looking vacantly before him, he implores your forgiveness," Neha said.

He could sense she was teary-eyed, something uncharacteristic in his family. All of a sudden, Vivek felt a thawing within him. Praying to hold onto the rush of tender emotions, he said with an affected coolness, "Okay, I'll do my best." He paused and brooded over his words. Then, after a short deliberation, he said with a sigh, "You win. I'll come. I promise."

"Thank you, Vivek." Her choked voice poured into his ears like molten lava.

He did go home, to find his mother and sister sitting next to each other before his father's lifeless body, wrapped in a crisp, white shroud and covered with garlands of marigold flowers. Extremely shocked, Vivek now did not know how to react. He was shaken and shattered. The sight of his widowed mother filled him with guilt. The whole thing only conveyed to him the frailty of human glory.

Overcome by sudden, impulsive grief, he fell upon the dead body of his father and, hugging it, cried out loudly, "Dad, don't lie over there with such indifference. Get up,

Dad! Your son has come! Now be good for once and talk to him!"

"Tame your grief, son. Your dad is gone. Wish him peace and say your last goodbye to him," his mother said, passing her hand tenderly over Vivek's head, trying to console him.

On hearing his mother's consoling words, Vivek was overcome by a surge of powerful emotions. He rested his head on her comforting bosom, where he felt he would be safe from the worst incursions of the hostile world. This seemed to blunt the wild edge of his grief.

All of a sudden, both of them burst into loud, spasmodic sobs.

As the days passed, slowly and steadily, the household started to return to normalcy. In the month since his father's death, Vivek had hardly emerged from his room. He had spoken with his principal at university and had requested a month off, assuring him that he would make up for the semester by studying at home. The principal had been an old friend of Vivek's father. He generously agreed to the arrangement.

It was a tough period in Vivek's life. Mostly, he stayed in his own room. He felt for his mother, but he did not know how to console her. She, too, was going through great emotional turmoil. After a long period of deliberation, he thought it would be better to let her deal with her grief on her own and come to terms with life. During this period, he also noticed his sister taking particular care of their mother. She would sit with her in the lawn in the evenings and read the newspaper out loud to her in order to distract her. In the mornings, she would take her out for walks and try to chat with her. All day long, she would come up with some activity or the other that would include their mother and keep her busy. Vivek knew Neha was trying her best to make their mother realize that life had to go on and that it was not the end for her yet.

He was relieved and also somewhat ashamed that his sister was succeeding at something that he failed at. He knew that the relations between the two of them were as strained as those between him and his mother, but Neha was intelligent and sympathetic enough in that hour to put everything behind her and start afresh. Maybe her marriage had something to do with it. Girls usually come closer to their parents once they get married and go away. They become more concerned. Whatever the explanation, he was happy to see them like that and knew it was time for him to go back and get on with his studies.

Before he left, his uncle called him over for a talk.

"Vivek, you had better join the family business," Vivek's uncle told him.

"I can't."

"Why?"

"I've to complete my studies."

"That's ridiculous."

"Why is it ridiculous?"

"Your father's position must be filled. We can't let the vacuum affect the business," said his uncle.

"Bullshit."

"What do you mean by that?"

"First, you make what you want clear."

"I mean join the business and work the way your father did, as the business will be affected otherwise," the uncle explained.

"I don't believe you, *Chachu*. You are actually talking of finding a replacement for your brother!" said Vivek rather bluntly.

"Don't be stupid, Vivek! Who said I was looking for his replacement? And do not forget, your father was my brother, too!"

"Yeah, a brother who was no good to you except as a person who could mint money and so, even at this sensitive time, all you are bothered about is business and money."

"Shut up, Vivek. That's the worst accusation! I'm hurt!" the uncle said, as if he had been grievously wronged.

A bitter smile came to Vivek's face. Fixing his gaze upon his uncle, he said, "Understand one thing very clearly, *Chachu*. Under no circumstances am I going to give up my studies."

"Aren't you concerned in the least about the family business?"

Vivek could not control himself anymore. He said, "What family? A brother who is keen to find a replacement for his partner? I am not interested in being a part of such a setup. Besides, I don't think I can take the business forward like my father did, so you please manage it on your own."

Flying off the handle, his uncle retorted, "I think your father was right in calling you a lost soul, Vivek. You don't yourself know what you are saying and why you hold so much of a grudge against us all. Anyway, I am not interested in explaining things to you or talking to you about what I think of your father. I asked you to join the business as I thought you would realize that you have a responsibility towards this house and your family. If you wish to stay aloof, do that by all means."

"I know what my responsibilities are and will also take care of them when the need arises," Vivek said in a cool voice.

"Well, if you think the time is not ripe yet, then only God can save your soul."

Vivek had made his intentions clear to his uncle, who made it clear that Vivek's share would be transferred into his bank account. This was a source of immense relief to Vivek. He did not have a good opinion of his uncle and he didn't want to have any association with a person who could look for a replacement for his own brother and had never had any concern for his nephew. It was an important realization—another step in knowing about the ways of the world.

"I am leaving tomorrow morning, Ma," Vivek told his mother.

"Okay."

"I hope you know that *Chachu* has asked me to join the business but I refused as I have no interest in it. He then offered to give me my share of the money from it."

"So, what have you decided?"

"I don't need the money. Whatever my share is, I will transfer it to your and Neha's accounts. The two of you will not have any problems in the future and will be financially secure."

"We don't need that, son. We are going to be taken care of. Your father has left me so much that I do not have to worry about anything. You have a life ahead, so focus on that."

"But what will I do with so much?"

"It is not much. Keep it with you and use it at the right time. Life without money can be difficult. Your father would have liked you to join the business, but I won't force you into it now. It is your life and your decision."

"Yeah, my life and my decision. Anyway, I have a lot to cover up as far as my studies are concerned, so I will be leaving tomorrow. I have my semester exams coming up next month and I do not want to lag behind."

"When will you come next?"

"I just told you, Ma, I have lot of catching up to do and my exams…"

"Take care of yourself and do not stress too much. Things will be fine here soon. I will be alright, too, in some time."

"I will call you regularly and, if you need anything, let me know."

"Vivek," his mother whispered.

"Yes, Ma?"

"I love you."

"You don't have to tell me that."

"Since you're going away, I want to tell you something."

"Ma, I'm your son. You don't have to hesitate before me."

"There are moments when I feel I haven't been a good mother."

"Why do you say that? I don't accept it."

"But it's the truth."

"How so?"

"I followed my ambitions so much that I overlooked my motherly duties."

Her words touched Vivek. She wasn't someone who could easily talk of emotions in general and regrets and mistakes in particular. It must have taken a lot of courage for her to admit this. Overcome, he said, "Ma, your son is just going away on a bigger mission. He'll come back soon."

Her face beamed with happiness. "I want to tell you something else, too."

"What is it?"

"Money and success do not make a man great." She paused and focused her gaze upon her son. Then, at the end of a long pause, she said, "I want you to rise above your petty ends." She stopped again.

He looked at her curiously.

She went on, "This country will wake up when its youth wakes up. Don't fritter away your life in pursuit of vanities."

"I won't Ma. I won't," he promised.

"Blessings, my son. May you be the happiest person on earth."

He left the place with a new determination. Things had changed. He now had two big fixed deposits and complete freedom. He felt as if he had been released from a dark, dingy room. No more did he find himself gripped in the talons of claustrophobia. Refreshed, he began enjoying his hostel life.

Memories overlapped…

The horn of a motorbike suddenly made Vivek realize that he had been staring at the STD booth for over half an hour now. He decided to come back later to undertake the task of calling home. The process of going into the past and recounting those horrible days had left him drained. He just wanted to go back to his room and sleep again. Besides, the sunny afternoon was too much for him to bear. *A cool glass of lemonade or even water will calm my flared nerves*, he thought.

He proceeded towards a vendor selling fresh lemonade, which was stored in a clay pot. The earthiness of the pot added a new dimension to the flavor of the lemonade and the mint leaves in it soothed his throat and mind. *This is the flavor of true India*, he thought.

While sipping the cool water, he saw that the vendor was trying to shoo away a little girl of seven or eight. She, however, was adamant in wanting his attention. She had a little broken slate in her hand and was speaking in rapid Gujarati. Although he did know the language, it was difficult for him to understand the quick words that were emerging from the child's mouth.

"What does she want?" he asked.

"Oh, nothing, *sahib*," said the vendor.

"She clearly needs your attention. Is it about the slate? Something she has written?"

"Her slate is broken. There are many in her school who either don't have slates or have really old, broken ones. She's no different, *sahib*. That's what I'm trying to tell her."

"But that's not right. Which school does she go to?"

"It's the government primary school for girls here, *sahib*. Just around the corner."

"Everyone deserves to study, *bhai*. Don't put it in your own daughter's head that her education is dispensable."

Thoughtful, Vivek made his way back to Paresh's home. As soon as he reached the open area adjoining the bungalow, he noticed that a crowd had gathered outside it. Worried that something untoward had happened, he quickly ran towards the house. The moment he reached the gate, he noticed Paresh and his entire family seated in the verandah with their neighbors consoling them. He opened the gate and entered, huffing and puffing because of the short sprint he had attempted.

"What happened? Is everything all right?" he asked.

Hearing his voice in the crowd, Paresh looked up to see Vivek standing right next to him. Breaking into a cry, Paresh cried, "*Babuji*! Where had you gone? You had us all so worried! We thought you had left because there was something you didn't like about us or our way of life. We really were saddened by your disappearance!"

Realizing that he had become a reason for commotion and chaos in the simple lives of his benefactors, Vivek apologetically said, "I'm extremely sorry if that was what you thought. I had just gone to the market to have breakfast and get some sweets for you people. I didn't know that you would get so worried."

"*Arre, babuji,* why are you apologizing? And why did you go out to get yourself breakfast? Why didn't you tell Raju?"

Paresh then turned towards his son and started scolding him. Looking at the cluelessness with which Rajesh was staring back at his father, Vivek stepped in to rescue him and said, "Don't scold Raju, Paresh. He has got nothing to do with any of this. When I got up around noon, I saw no one was at home, so I decided to step out and take a stroll and also to have breakfast. Simple. There's no need to make an issue of the whole situation. I think I'm grown up enough to take care of myself, so you don't have to get this worried about things. Now, come on, let us all go inside. It is getting too hot outside for me to bear."

The family thanked the neighbors for coming to console them and, after introducing them to Vivek, saw them off at the gate.

Realizing the matter had been settled, Vivek then said, "Look what I got for you all: *jalebis.* I had a scrumptious breakfast of *kachoris* and *jalebis* and thought of bringing some back for you all. Hope you enjoy it."

"Of course, *babuji,* we all love *jalebis.*"

Paresh then told Neelu to make tea for them as they made their way to the dining-cum-living room. Over tea, they spent the evening talking about the town and its development and Paresh's plans for Pooja and Rajesh. Vivek felt his determination to do something about the lemonade vendor's little girl (and the others in her school) growing.

The very next day, he visited the school and was soon busy acquiring basic amenities and getting them sent there.

*****

Days passed. Vivek had settled well into his new environment. He loved every moment spent not doing much. He would get up around seven in the morning and go for a walk in the green fields adjoining the house. Then, after having a bath, he would again go for a stroll in the town, eat something at his favorite vendor's stall, go through a newspaper at a tea shop and finally come back home.

He loved observing Paresh's everyday activities; Vivek had never seen anyone live like him before. His lifestyle was unique, heartwarming and intriguing. The first thing he would in the morning was go touch the photographs of his parents and grandparents on the walls of the corridors around the courtyard, as if touching their feet.

When Vivek asked him about it, Paresh said, "*Babuji*, I would not be anything without them. I would not be. Isn't it only natural for me to remember and thank them for this precious gift before I start my day?"

As always, with a tiny look into Paresh's simple world, Vivek felt enormously envious of what he could never have.

On one occasion, Vivek went to Paresh's shop. Paresh, busy making *samosas*, saw Vivek standing outside the place.

"Please, be seated, *babuji*," he said, pointing towards a bench. Then, turning to his assistant, he said, "Bring two *samosas*."

When the *samosas* arrived, Vivek protested, "There're too big, I can't have two at a time!"

"Please have them. They are two different types of *samosas*. One is a paneer *samosa* and the other one is mixed vegetable *samosa*," said Paresh with pride. "These're very light on the stomach."

"They're fantastic," said Vivek, after taking a big bite out of each one.

"*Babuji*, trust me," said Paresh, "I can make a hundred kinds of *samosas*, that too in different shapes and sizes. It's our national heritage, after all."

Taking another bite, Vivek said, "You must make many more kinds of *samosas*. That's my suggestion to you. It'll make you an internationally popular *samosa*-maker. I know you can't sell a variety of samosas daily at your railway station, but you can certainly organize *samosa* festivals in different places from time to time. As you've said, it's a national heritage."

Paresh burst into laughter. "Thank you, *babuji*, for your appreciation. But I can't dream of those things. They are beyond my wildest imagination."

There was so much to learn from Paresh and his family. They left seeds and water out for birds, kept water outside their main gate for cows and dogs and took turns leaving *chapattis* and vegetable scraps for cows and other animals, even ants. Vivek found all this fascinating, and what deepened his feelings for the family even further was the rationale that guided Paresh: "Our world is like a chain, *babuji*. We receive, we give. What we give always comes back. I feel that this is the best lesson I can teach my children. All of the other lessons they will receive from the world. But if they know and remember and follow this *sanskar*, nothing will ever break them. Just like you gave so much to the girls' school. Don't think I don't know. People talk about you with immense gratitude and affection. In such a short time, you have won so many hearts. That is another example of the chain of goodness."

Vivek found little things all around him in the house that were constant reminders of what he had never had but could perhaps have created if someone had been there to guide him. He felt that Paresh and his family were really fortunate to have each other. They knew how to live life with immense calm and contentment. Evidence of satisfied living was present everywhere, all the time. This rubbed off on him and he began to relax and find satisfaction, too. Although electricity was scarce, with no air conditioning nor any of the other comforts Vivek was otherwise used to, life never seemed difficult. He never felt any kind of discomfort. To him, it was like life in that part of the world was all about taking it easy. People here did not wallow in regret over little things, as they had grown up without many amenities. So, for them, whatever was available was good enough. They did not crib about not having enough water or electricity.

Paresh and his wife used to leave for their shop at around eight in the morning and toil all day long to meet the supply requirements. Neelu would cook food on returning from work and the entire family would sit in the verandah and have dinner.

A Glimpse of a New Lifestyle

Vivek had begun to offer his assistance to Pooja and Rajesh with their homework and to teach them English, political science and economics, as he felt that children, especially those coming from small towns, did not have sufficient exposure to books and other materials that would make them aware of the world beyond their immediate surroundings. In a matter of a few days, he discovered that the boy had a streak of genius in matters of mathematics and science and the girl was keen on social science and history. Vivek wanted to help them advance in their respective areas of interest.

"Your grades seem to be improving by the day, Raju," Paresh said to his son one day.

"Papa, it is all thanks to Uncle Vivek," said Rajesh.

"Yes, the amount of hard work he puts into taming a monkey like you is commendable."

"Papa, don't call me that. Look, my marks are good now. You should not say these things anymore."

"If you continue to perform like this then I will surely stop calling you that. Now, go and study harder. You have to uphold not just my honor but also Vivek *babuji's*. After all, he has put in so much hard work."

"*Ji*, Papa."

When no one was home, Vivek would go out and take long strolls, often coming face-to-face with the innocence of the residents of the town and their approach to life, which was open and progressive compared to the approach prevailing in the metros.

During one of his evening walks, he came across a group of women sitting by a tube well. They seemed to belong to lower middle class families and had gathered there, which he assumed was their daily meeting point, to sit, chat and indulge in humorous banter and gossip about everything under the sun. Vivek knew he was guilty of eavesdropping on their conversation, but he found the entire process and the way they behaved with each other so amusing that he decided to sit there and listen to them.

"Mynah, your kid is hungry!" the oldest person in the group jokingly said to a rather young mother in her early 20s who was busy trying to pacify her weeping few-months-old kid.

"He's always hungry, *didi*," replied Mynah.

Another enthusiastic lady from the group said, "You must feed him properly."

"*Arre*, I fed him banana paste before coming here! It hasn't been very long since. What is the little devil crying about? He's always hungry!"

Another woman cheekily said, "He must be craving your milk. These kids, I tell you, especially boys, are always crying for their mother's milk. Mine was three years old when I forcibly rid him of the habit of asking for my milk."

"Men and their obsession with female breasts! I guess it starts from early age," said another.

The entire group burst into laughter. Their bold conversation, laced with sexual innuendo, both shocked and amused Vivek. He knew that women who were educated talked about such things in posh cafes and bistros, but the fact that women who belonged to lower strata of society also did so opened Vivek's eyes to the realization that people everywhere were the same. Attitudes and behaviors changed in response to circumstances, but fundamentally all humans craved the same things.

Stepping away from his thoughts, he continued to concentrate on the conversation.

Mynah said, "Mine is a step ahead from yours in his naughtiness. Just the other day, he was sucking my breast so hard that he ended up biting my nipple. Such a cheeky bastard!"

The group burst into another round of chuckles. The woman who had started the conversation ordered Mynah to show them all her bite marks. Without a moment's hesitation, Mynah obeyed, unbuttoning her blouse to show them the proof. Vivek was taken back by Mynah's spontaneity and felt a bit embarrassed. *What a bold and brash woman she is*, he thought.

His thoughts then veered in the direction of the women he would often encounter at official parties in cities. He thought of how hard they tried to expose their bodies in short dresses and almost non-existent blouses to seduce men. And here was a group of women who were not even aware that such a species existed in the world. For them, it was all in the moment. They did not have double-standards like their city counterparts. They did not wear titillating clothes in their everyday life and, yet, were comfortable in their own skin and did not fuss over any of their body parts being exposed.

While the women's teasing continued, he heard one of the elderly ladies say to Mynah, "Are you sure these marks have been made by your son and not by someone else?"

"*Hai hai*, what do you mean? You think that some bug or an insect bit me here, out of all the available body parts?" Mynah retorted.

"No, I meant maybe a bigger bug. You know who I mean!" They all broke into laughter at the thought of Mynah's sexcapades with her husband.

To Vivek, the ways of the rich and the educated seemed to make less sense than those of the people beneath them in the social hierarchy. It would be considered immoral or obscene in a metropolitan city if a group of women behaved like these women. They would be reprimanded by the moral police and made to realize how wrong they were to engage in such sexually-charged interactions. But here, in this supposedly conservative small town, things, it seemed, were more relaxed and less open to scrutiny.

It had become a part of his everyday routine for Vivek to go on such strolls and discover a new facet of the people of the town, whom he otherwise felt very detached from. One day, he was walking by the river bank when he came across a woman bathing in the river. What caught his fancy was the way she was taking her bath. She had wrapped herself in a cotton sari and was washing only one half of the sari while the other half was clinging to her body. When she was done with washing one side, she wrapped the wet part around her body, unwrapped the dry part, and then started washing that. The incident reminded him of what Munshi Premchand had written in *Godan*—that in India, there is still a class of people who do not have enough to even clothe themselves properly. This woman was the perfect example of the India he had described. Vivek then began thinking, *what is the use of India progressing when its progress benefits only a few fortunate ones while the majority languish in obscurity and poverty?* Where was the India of his dreams, where everyone lived as equals and there were no social and economic barriers? Where the poor had as many opportunities available to them as the rich? Where all that mattered was the betterment of society, of people? He had no answers to these harrowing questions.

Earlier, work had hardly allowed him any time to relax with his family or go for walks. Over the years, he had put on a bit of weight and his waistline was now expanding at the same rate as his business. He would occasionally go to a nearby gym, but eventually his visits became infrequent, as his business began taking a significant shape. So, obviously, he was now happy to see all that extra fat vanishing from his body thanks to these strolls; in a way, these walks were motivating him to stay fit and healthy.

During another such stroll, Vivek decided to visit Paresh's establishment. An idea had been taking shape in his mind for a few days. He was thinking of utilizing his knowledge of business and his professional experience to help Paresh expand his reach and transform him into a business-savvy person. He had seen how kind and righteous Paresh was as a person and also knew that, due to his humble upbringing, he would always be hesitant to take major risks in life.

"*Arre babuji*, what are you doing here?"

"I was just passing by, so I thought I would drop by to taste another one of your famous *samosas*."

"*Arre*, you could have told me earlier, I would have brought them home for you. Why did you take the pain of coming all this way?"

"I wasn't doing anything at home, Paresh. Besides, I really wanted to see how you worked."

"Please come in and have a seat. I will ask someone to bring you water and *samosas*."

"So, how are things going today?"

"*Bas*, *babuji*, busy, like it is every day. Last evening there was a train accident because of which many trains got delayed. There is a huge rush at the railway station because of the delays, so the demand for *samosas* has also gone up."

"Is it a good or a bad situation? Paresh, have you never thought of going beyond this town? I mean, people the world over love to eat and experiment with food. India itself is so vast that anything and everything related to food sells. So why restrict yourself to just Divi and the railway station?"

"What are you saying, *babuji*. It is not for people like me to think so big. As long as I'm getting my two square meals a day and able to take good care of my family, I'm happy."

"I hope this thought has got nothing to do with living in a small world of your own and not risking venturing out?"

"*Babuji*, that may be the case, but there is also the fact that I am a man of humble means and happy to remain one. Some people, hardcore businessmen, see their own profits in any kind of human tragedy. I don't. I've got respect for any kind of life. For me, life is a sacred thing. It's a gift from God. If any life is destroyed in an accident, it can't be a source of personal gain."

"But stepping out of your comfort zone may not necessarily mean losing out on anything. Who knows, maybe you will end up gaining a lot."

"*Babuji*, frankly speaking, I am happy where I am. I am a *samosa* maker and not a dreamer. I am well-connected with my reality and am happy to live the way I do."

This little conversation with Paresh gave Vivek the impression that, even though Paresh would like to get out of the mundane life that he and his family were living, as a common man, he was too scared to try. Paresh had dared only once, when he had thought of setting up this small business. He had just enough confidence in himself to take daily risks related to his work, but nothing more. Vivek knew that a bit of push could make Paresh more confident of his own skills and talent. Maybe at this point in time he was not looking at making Paresh a behemoth in his line, but yes, to start with, a better setup and better packaging of the product would be good enough to get more eyeballs on the already locally famous Matru ka Samosa.

He thought that, since Paresh had helped him so much and had literally entered his life like an angel and helped him choose the right path when he had thought it was all over, he owed this much to him. He was now planning to invest all his knowledge in Paresh's business and was slowly gaining the determination to make him a big man, worthy of his talent and stature. He remembered the conversation he had had with Paresh over a cup of evening tea and *mathri* with lemon pickle. He had then asked Paresh about his future plans for himself and his business and how he wanted the careers of his children to shape up. Paresh had replied that, although he had had to struggle a lot all through his childhood to reach where he was, he wanted to provide his children with an easier and more fulfilling life. He said that he wanted his children to study and become good and knowledgeable individuals. He wanted them to be worthy of bringing change to the town they had grown up in, so that there would be more like them who would be inspired to do the same and helped Divi prosper and progress.

Paresh had created an exclusive atmosphere in his home for Vivek. Silently, Vivek appreciated his thoughtfulness, but he was convinced that Paresh did not have much insight into the real functioning and the complex nature of modern finances. But he was in for a major surprise.

One day, he and Paresh were talking.

"Paresh, you must put everything in a broader context now," Vivek told Paresh.

"You're right, *babuji*! I don't have your kind of vision and wisdom."

"You must think about the future of the children, too. I want to give you some ideas and help you make some plans for the future of your children," said Vivek with confidence.

Paresh flashed his typical smile, then said, "*Babuji*, never make the mistake of overlooking the truth that, even though I'm just a small-time *samosa* maker in a small town, I am always thinking about the well-being of my children."

"That's great, Paresh, I'm happy to hear it. But do share your thoughts with me. I might be of some help, too," said Vivek reassuringly.

"*Babuji*, I read the Hindi newspaper every day. I listen to the news on electronic media. Then I form my own strategy."

"What do you think of the economic trends today?"

"My first impression is that one should be very transparent about one's finances today. *Babuji*, you'll be happy to know that I'm a regular taxpayer. All my money, each and every penny, and all my properties are clearly accounted for in my tax declarations."

"That's the best thing to do," Vivek said appreciatively.

"There is one more thing I'd like to tell you," Paresh said in a low voice.

"Yes, go ahead, Paresh."

"Investment is the best option today. In my opinion, it's the way to prosperity. In the past, people kept their money at home. It reduced in value with the passing of time. So, I invest my money in different sectors."

Vivek was impressed with the financial wisdom of this simple man. Paresh was a genius; he understood contemporary trends better than most scholars.

Paresh continued, "I have insurances and fixed deposits in the names of my children, so they will keep getting a regular income for several years after turning 25. I've also made some educational investments and taken a wedding insurance policy for them. The insurance in my daughter's name will mature by the time she is marriageable, and I'm sure it'll make her life hassle-free at a certain level."

"Paresh, I never thought that you would have such brilliant insights into such a complex subject," said Vivek, reaching out to hold Paresh's hand warmly.

Paresh went on, "Besides these, I've invested my money in land, too. Not only in cities nearby, but also in cities a little further away. In my view, land is a very safe investment. *Babuji*, I invest money in land only when I know the government is planning to invest in infrastructure around that area in a big way. Any investment in land multiplies, in my experience. Buying land in small towns will be very profitable in the long run—a real bonanza!"

"I'm very happy you have been doing these things wisely and systematically," Vivek said, in genuine appreciation.

"Thank you! It's because of my well-wishers, *babuji*. It's with their blessings and wise mentoring that I stand on firm ground today," said Paresh humbly.

"Credit also goes to you, for your hard work and willingness to learn new things," said Vivek, continuing to hold his friend's hands warmly in his own.

"I've invested money in shares of big companies too. I bought some 300 shares of Maruti 10 years back at Rs. 300 per share; now, each share has risen up to the value of Rs. 9,000. I've invested money in blue-chip companies on the stock market, too."

"Blue-chip companies? What a surprise! Who told you about that?"

Paresh did not answer Vivek's question immediately. He paused and brooded over what he was going to say for a few seconds. "*Babuji*, I must tell you the truth. I'm not that wise.

In fact, a professor of economics loves my *samosas*. He is my mentor at several levels. His advice has given me stability. He has taught me how to invest astutely and properly. But, in the end, I use my discretion. My instinct for survival gives me the ultimate guidance. It tells me what's good or bad for me."

"I see the makings of a business magnate in you, my dear friend," said Vivek.

Paresh was on a roll. "I've made gold investments too, through an approved gold agency. I've invested it in 100-gram gold coins. Now I feel free and relaxed."

"By gosh, you're a wizard! A financial wizard, Paresh! Investment in gold too!" Vivek exclaimed.

Paresh smiled. He said, "*Babuji*, gold has historically been the safest of all investments. It'll always return 10% per annum, and sometimes, over shorter periods, it may go over 30–35%! Where else do you get such high returns? Besides that, when my daughter and son get married, if I'm short of cash, gold may be converted into jewelry items for my children."

"I understand my fault in thinking you had something to learn from me," said Vivek.

"No, no, *babuji*. There is a lot I can learn from you. But I have learned some things from elsewhere as well. I told you all of this to help you understand that I have the best interests of my family in mind. For that, I will learn everything I can."

"I'm sure you have taken care of everything, Paresh," said Vivek with admiration.

"*Babuji*, I want a happy married life for my daughter. But I want her to be educated first so that she does not become a liability to anyone. Not even her husband."

"It is good to know you think like this, Paresh."

"I want her to be smart and independent like those big town girls. You know, the ones who go to work and also take care of their family."

"But will you find such an open-minded family for her in Divi or in nearby areas?"

"For my daughter? I will go all out to find her a suitable match. I do not want her to stay in Divi all her life. It is not a place where she can fulfill her dreams."

"Are you ready to send her to the city for higher studies?"

"Of course, *babuji*. If need be, I will do that as well. I am not the kind who thinks girls should be married the moment they are done with their basic studies. I want my daughter to study as much as she wants. And marriages are all made in heaven. When the time is ripe, it will all fall in place."

Retrospection

When it came to the future of his children and money matters, Paresh was no novice. Vivek now realized that Paresh's business sense was great and that he was a good planner. He had tried to understand the economics of Paresh's business. Paresh told him that he sold close to 5,000 *samosas* a day at a price of Rs. 10 each, out of which he was able to make a rupee from each *samosa* after deducting all expenses. This meant, he was earning about Rs. 1,50,000 a month. Of this total amount, 75% went into his savings and the rest he utilized to run daily errands at home. So, overall, Paresh was doing well, considering the standards he was maintaining at home and at his shop and for the purposes of a town like Divi.

He had planned everything well in advance so that in the future, if any need arose, he would know what to do and how. He was an independent operator and therefore trusted his own instinct. He knew that one day his children would outgrow the desires he had in mind for them and would form their own opinions and likings, but he wanted to support them. The business that he currently had was good enough for him. Paresh was of the opinion that a man should stretch himself within the limits of his capacity. It was not advisable to give in to greed and lose everything in the desire to earn more. He knew that, at this point in time, he had the means and caliber to cater to the needs of just three shops in Ankleshwar, five important railway stations between Ankleshwar and Ahmedabad and five important railway stations on the Ankeleshwar–Mumbai route. His *samosas* were so popular that passengers of all the trains passing through these stations rushed to get "four pieces of 'Matru ka *samosa!*'" He did want to expand his business and had ambitions of making it big for the sake of his family, but he was also wise enough to know that he did not have the resources to fuel his ambition.

Also, growth would require him to invest more time and money and that would mean compromising on his family time. To him, family meant everything. It was bigger than money or anything else in the world. His sole desire was to see them happy and he knew that, with the business in its present condition, he was in a position to fulfill their wishes and wants. He was indeed a very practical man and was always prepared for tough times. As a person, he was magnanimous. He had a desire to do something for the people of his town. He wanted to employ more and more people and provide them with opportunities to grow. He wanted to enhance their talent and skills so that they could be self-reliant. He was a man of bigger ideas and motives, but of limited means and even more limited money.

Vivek appreciated the work-life balance that Paresh had been able to achieve and how balanced and objective a person he was. He knew what he wanted from his life and how he wanted to live it. The love he had for his children was the sole driving force of his life and everything revolved around it. He had noble ambitions, too, as he was considerate towards his town people and wanted to do something that would attract attention to his town and give its people an opportunity to become economically stronger. To him, business was business, but when he stepped out of his small shop, his life was all about family. A balance Vivek had never been able to strike, alas!

More memories. More retrospection.

Vivek, from the very beginning, had been unidimensional. For him, the sole aim in life was to just be by himself. His eccentricities had cost him a lot and only when he had reached Divi and experienced life on the other side had he realized how hollow and empty his existence had been until then. The trappings of his eccentric life were catching up with him and, by living there with Paresh and his family, he had started to realize that, if only he had lived life differently, things would have been simpler and he happier.

In college, when his friends would go out for movies or dinner and drinks, he would prefer to stay back in his hostel room and either study or while away his time doing nothing. He had never bunked classes or sat in the canteen engaging in random chitchat. For him, hostel was an escape from his life at home, but even there he lived a trapped life.

When, one fine day, Reeta walked into his life, he felt genuinely happy and relaxed. She was like a breath of fresh air, everything that he was not, and maybe that was why he felt instantly attracted to her when he was introduced to her by a common friend at their college fest. At first, he found her talkative nature a bit too much to handle, but the moment he realized that it was easier for him that way, as she was filling up all the long, silent gaps between them with her non-stop chatter, he started appreciating it. Within a matter of a few weeks, they had become very close, so much so that Vivek had started going out for movies and parties with her.

Reeta was the livewire daughter of a famous business tycoon. She had style and panache and, most importantly, money that could buy her anything and everything she desired. She knew that most people were attracted to her because of her family background and the money it promised, but she was wise enough not to make every person her friend. She was very beautiful, a girl who had the kind of charm that would sweep any man off his feet. But, for Vivek, money and power hardly ever had a magnetic effect. These were the very things he had detested right from the beginning of his life and was running away from all the time. Since he himself was born into riches, those things hardly mattered to him. And perhaps that was why even Reeta felt an instant attraction towards him at their very first meeting, as she felt that he was genuine and definitely not the sort to befriend people because they had money written all over their face.

"You know, Vivek, a lot of people befriend me for various reasons, but they all have one thing in common," she told him.

"What?"

"Their love for my money."

"You think so? Are you saying that people just fail to understand your true intentions? Come on, Reeta. Not everyone you meet can be so shallow."

"I didn't say all, I said most men."

"Maybe you think this because so far you have not really met the right kind of men."

"How can you be sure of that?"

"Well, because I do not fall into the category of such men. I don't care about money and have struck up a friendship with you not because you are rich or anything like that, but because I genuinely like you as a person."

"You do?"

"Of course. I value you as a person. Why else do you think I would be wasting my time sitting here and talking with you?"

"You're being rude, Vivek."

"No, I am telling you the truth. You don't have to compartmentalize people. Maybe some of them genuinely have been attracted to you, but you have this preconceived notion in your mind."

"Maybe you are right. But it really is difficult for me to judge who is genuine and who is fake."

"Then stop judging people. Accept them for who they are and not for who you would want them to eventually be."

"I guess you are right. I should really not put so much thought into things like these. I think there are many things of more importance that I need to concentrate on right now."

"Exactly."

Over a period of time, Vivek had genuinely started caring for Reeta. He would think about her and make plans for their dates well in advance. Every evening, after college, he would look forward to meeting her over a cup of coffee or going on long drives in her car to areas adjoining Delhi. During one such night of drunken revelry, they had almost driven to Jaipur. It was only when they realized they had been out together for too long and Vivek remembered he had an important project to submit the next morning that they sped back. They realized it had been stupid on their part, but for the next few days they had a good laugh over it every time they discussed it among themselves or with their friends. Vivek had never experienced this side of life and so he was trying to make the most of every bit of it.

After meeting Reeta, there was a marked changed in his attitude too. He would call his mother regularly, every second day, and most of the time he would talk about Reeta. Becoming aware of her son's fondness for this new girl in his life and his change in attitude, Vivek's mother decided to call them over for dinner one day. Nervous, yet proud of his choice, Vivek arrived with Reeta. He had told his mother that he did not wish to introduce Reeta to his uncle as he did not feel comfortable in his company.

His mother had made arrangements for dinner in her part of the bungalow. The bungalow in which Vivek had grown up was a huge palatial affair. It had two wings, with a huge lawn in between them. Vivek used to live with his parents and sister in the rear wing of the bungalow while his uncle and his family occupied the front part. The family had separated years ago.

As a kid, Vivek had once heard a conversation between his father and mother during which his mother was insistent on living separately from the others, as she could not cope with the joint family system. She had problems with her sister-in-law, too, and was fed up of her habit of picking fights over the slightest of things and then prolonging it for hours. Vivek's mother lived a very busy life and, after returning from a long day of spending time listening to the daily predicaments of strangers and counselling them on ways to sort out their problems, she was unable to control the situation at home.

She would at times just walk away from a conversation when it got too much for her to digest. Finally, one day, she told Adarsh that she was losing it with her sister-in-law and, if he did not take the decision to separate, she would walk out of the house. Adarsh was at first devastated, but after much deliberation, and having tried and failed to convince her to back down, he relented, and soon, within a few days, the two families were divided into two houses. Since Vivek's grandfather was not in favor of one family going away and living separately, the house itself was sacrificed, rather than the humans living inside it. *Daduji* decided that, of the two wings of the house, one each would be occupied by one family and he would continue to live in the front wing. Since Vivek's mother was adamant about having no interference in her everyday life, Adarsh agreed on the rear wing of the house, as it would mean his father would not be able to keep an eye on her or poke his nose in her affairs. Vivek was too young for the situation to register or have an impact on him. As he was cut off from most of the family anyway, it did not bother him much. The only thing that hit him hard was that, every time he wanted to play with his cousins, he had to ask permission from his mother, which he found tedious. In fact, he completely stopped going out because it would mean approaching his mother and asking for permission. Slowly and gradually, it created a rift between the cousins and, with the passage of time, they lost touch with each other. On occasion, they would exchange a few words of courtesy, but for the most part they knew nothing about each other. The decision to separate had not only destroyed the equation between the family members but also the whole notion of a happy and loving joint family.

The house had a small pond, too, with a variety of fish swimming in it. It was a beautiful house, lined with mango and *jamun* trees. As a child, during the summer vacations, Vivek used to climb up the mango tree and spend almost his entire day eating the fruit, plucked fresh from the tree.

Reeta was impressed with the very first look of Vivek's house. She had never seen such a calm and serene house and so she took an instant liking to it.

"What a beautiful house you have, Vivek! I have never seen anything like this before!"

After entering the compound, Vivek drove to the back of the bungalow, trying his best to avoid any sort of contact with his uncle or his family. His mother greeted them at the entrance and a quick round of introductions was made.

"Ma, this is Reeta."

"*Namaste*, aunty."

"Oh, come on in, *beta*. I have been waiting for you two for quite a while now. What took you so long?"

"We got caught in a traffic jam, Ma. You know how the traffic situation in our city is," Vivek said as they proceeded inside.

The interior of the house was a vision of elegance. Big French windows, walls decorated with beautiful paintings and exquisite furnishings and handcrafted decorative pieces sourced from all over the world added a Victorian charm to the house. Reeta observed everything carefully. As she herself was interested in interior decoration, she thought that, if ever she had a house of her own, she would like to model it after Vivek's house. They all finally sat down in the living room to chat.

The mother spoke first. "Reeta, over the past few days Vivek has spoken so much about you over the phone that I could not resist meeting you in person and so decided to call you two over for dinner."

Feeling embarrassed by his mother's proclamation of his infatuation in front of Reeta, Vivek blushingly said, "Ma, I think we should talk about other stuff, too, besides Reeta."

Proud of being the object of Vivek's attention, Reeta was filled with love for him in that moment. She looked at him with her eyes wide open, as though silently trying to convey to him that she had been unaware until then that he liked her enough to talk about her with a mother he was not even that close to.

Blushing, she said, "Aunty, it's very sweet of Vivek to do that and I'm really happy to be here with you tonight. By the way, I have to add that you have a taste for finer things in life and this house is really like a beautiful piece of art!"

"Thank you, *beta*. Vivek's father and I were fond of travelling, so whenever he used to get free time from his business, we would visit places in India and abroad. I have picked up most of these items from my trips to different places. I'm glad you like it all."

The topic then moved towards asking Reeta's family, her background, what she was currently studying, her future plans and other things. The lovingness and affection with which

Reeta spoke to his mother impressed Vivek. He knew his mother was a difficult person to please, as she did not warm to people easily. But with Reeta, she seemed comfortable and was talking about things she normally would not bring up with him or with anyone she was meeting for the first time.

A thought struck Vivek. If he were to marry Reeta, maybe his mother would be happy and not throw tantrums. Maybe Reeta could change the equations people shared with each other in this family and eventually become the binding agent. He quickly brushed away the thought, as he felt it was a bit too early for him to think of marriage and what it could lead to. He had just met her and he did not even know if Reeta reciprocated his feelings. When his trail of thought was broken, he realized they were discussing Reeta's future plans. He told his mother about how she planned to open her own interior design studio, where she would handle only rich clients. Reeta told her that, since her father held a position of repute in the country, it would not be difficult for her to initially take support from him and then move on to establish an identity of her own.

Impressed with Reeta's plans and her need to be independent, Vivek's mother said, "I'm very happy to know that you think like this, *beta*. Girls, especially those from the kind of background that you come from, do not really feel the need to have an identity of their own. You seem a different sort and I hope that you do succeed in whatever you wish to do in life."

With that, Vivek's mother excused herself for few minutes to go and check if dinner was ready. She left the two of them alone in the room to enjoy each other's company. But Vivek felt quite awkward and at a loss for words. He did not know what to say to Reeta. He just looked around. He felt as if he was seeing that room for the first time in his life.

To break the silence, Reeta made the first move. She said, "So, you talk about me with your mother? I didn't know that." She winked at Vivek in a flirtatious manner.

"*Arre*, nothing like that, *yaar*. You know how mothers are. They have this habit of exaggerating things. She was just pulling my leg in front of you," said Vivek, embarrassed.

"I know your mother is not that kind of person, Vivek. What is the harm in admitting that you do talk about me? Anyway, if you can't say it then I will—I do like you a lot and think about you all the time. In fact, the only reason I agreed to come with you to this dinner and to meet your mother was because I thought it was time we took our relationship to the next level."

Taken aback by Reeta's frankness and the unabashed expression of her feelings, Vivek was left tongue-tied. He found himself speechless, as he was not prepared for the situation, but decided that he must reply to her by choosing his words carefully and wisely. Both Reeta and his emotions and sentiments were at stake. He did not wish to hurt her feelings and so, after much struggle, said, "Reeta, yes, I think I do genuinely like you, but right now I'm a little confused about my feelings for you. I mean…I'm not saying I won't talk to you after today or anything like that. In fact, I owe you a lot for making me the person I have become of late: outgoing, more social, happy. It has all been possible because of you. But I need time to think before taking the next big step."

He could see disappointment written all over Reeta's face and that glow of love suddenly vanishing. It broke his heart to see that he had yet again become the reason for someone's unhappiness and wanted to kill himself for doing that to Reeta. But he had no choice. To console her and to brighten her mood, he said, slowly but clearly, "I'm just asking you for a little time. I'm not saying I want to get away from you. You're the only person in my life I can share my dreams with. So please support me and don't react like this. Trust me! In a matter of few days, it will be all right, and I'm sure you, too, will appreciate later in life what I'm trying to do right now. Also, I have plans for my post-graduation and want to concentrate on getting into IIM."

"This is very disappointing!"

"What's disappointing?"

"Your putting the issue off for so many years! What's the need?"

"I've already told you!"

"It suggests something else."

"What?"

"You won't like it."

"Don't worry about that, go on," Vivek insisted.

"It's quite unpredictable at times," said Reeta, her eyes shining strangely. "I take fast decisions. You seem a slow guy!"

"I refuse to accept that."

"This is my impression," said Reeta emphatically. He looked at her closely this time. A smile came over her face. "You're headstrong too!"

"You're being harsh," he said.

Changing the topic, she observed, "Your mom is a wonderful person. I feel I've fallen in love with her!"

Vivek said, "She is a great charmer. Everyone is impressed by her! She is a perfect social being and, yet, on certain issues she is adamant. That annoys me."

She laughed. He looked at her questioningly.

She explained, "Any kind of rigidity hurts a person."

Getting back to the topic, Vivek said, "Okay then, it's fixed. We must give it some time. Right?"

Reeta said, "Okay! I think you are right. Both of us should take some more time before making any big decisions. And, also, you will have to meet my dad first and only then can we take things further."

Vivek laughed. "You're a dear girl. So perceptive. As you say, madame." They laughed out loud.

Vivek's mother called out to them. Dinner was ready.

Disillusioned

Certain incidents and thoughts should be left frozen in one's mind so that, when needed, one can revisit those moments and live those happy times once again.

The time that followed with Reeta was beautiful, almost like a fairytale. It seemed that life was only about being together and enjoying each other's company. His post-graduation at IIM got over. Reeta's initial business setup had also taken on a satisfactory form. The time was ripe and they finally decided to take the plunge.

Their marriage was a lavish affair. Although Vivek was not very happy at the pomp and show that made it a kind of a spectacle, considering the reputations of his and Reeta's families, he could not do much to protest against it. The only bone of contention for Vivek was that he felt squandering a lot of money on a thing like marriage ceremonies was a complete waste. He would have preferred to give the amount spent on his wedding to a charity, as there are many people in the country who could have lived several lifetimes on the amount. For him, simplicity in things mattered more than anything else and a court marriage would have been the ideal choice. But due to pressure from both sides, he had no choice but to relent. Exotic food from various parts of the world was served, flowers were especially flown in from Thailand and the ceremonies stretched on for five days. It was a sheer show of power and money and Vivek was not at all pleased with it.

The initial days of the marriage were filled with love, romance and fun. But as the effect of the "newly married" tag started to wear off, life became mundane. Both of them became busy with their respective fields of work. After a brief stint at HSBC, Vivek had made up his mind to get into something of his own. Two of his friends from IIM had started an automobile business, and he decided to join them as a partner. He had a 20% equity stake in the business and took up the position of Director. His initial takeaway amounted to about three lakhs a month, which was enough for a lavish lifestyle. But Vivek wasn't interested in materialistic things. Since his business was in its initial stages, he was required to spend long hours at his factory and the office. Days and nights would pass by with him conducting meetings with MDs of big MNCs and private companies. He would at times be required to fly abroad, while back home, Reeta would be busy with her interior decoration business.

Initially, Reeta had decided to put her work on the backburner for a few years, as she genuinely wanted to spend as much time as possible in Vivek's company. But his long days at the office and super busy schedule had taken its toll on their love life. Reeta used to feel neglected most of the time. Whenever she needed him, he was busy with his meetings. Alone at home with no company, she started to feel depressed and lonely. She was frustrated with her situation and soon in her marriage as well. She was a modern woman and could do lots with her own life, but she was stuck with the feeling of being unloved and bored.

Reeta wanted and needed her husband's attention and love, but all she had in the name of this marriage was the tag of being someone's wife, nothing more. She thought passing time in the company of friends would take her mind off negative thoughts, but that, too, was a temporary relief. Realizing she was just wasting her time waiting for Vivek to show up, she finally decided to get back to her work and start again from where she had left off. By now, Vivek's business had started gaining a strong footing, so he had begun to find some time off from his work. But it was a bit too late, as the tables had now turned. Reeta had a high-flying career ahead of her and at no point was she ready to sacrifice it again. Having a vocation of her own and not merely being someone's wife was important to her and, with her clients praising her work every passing day, her confidence had also gone up several notches. Vivek tried his best to persuade Reeta to take a break from her work so that they could spend some time together, but her professional demands were such that she could not. Vivek had already started to feel the distance between them. Not that he was blaming Reeta for it, as somewhere deep down inside him he knew that, to a large extent, he was the reason behind their crumbling marriage.

Reeta and Vivek drifted apart. They had begun fighting over trivial issues and had created a wall of misunderstanding between them.

"Your makeup looks a little vulgar today," Vivek once observed when they were preparing for leave for a party.

"Really?"

"Yes."

"I know why you think so."

"What's the reason?"

"It'll hurt you to hear it."

"No, it won't."

"You're jealous of me!"

"I'm jealous of *you*?" Vivek laughed sarcastically. Reeta's hostility was evident. "Ask anyone about it—you resemble a female monkey!"

"You're such an outdated guy! You seem to have been cut off from human emotions completely!" Reeta said bitterly. She paused briefly, casting around for words that would hurt and upset him. She eventually said in a cold, unfeeling way, "You've grown old prematurely. I'm sure of it. I put up with you for nothing! I can't tell others that you've lost the ability to be a husband."

For a few seconds, Vivek was hurt, but he collected himself. When he began again, his voice was very bitter. "You and your friends are just wayward vagabonds. As your minds are peanut-sized, you aren't even aware of what true elegance means. You aren't remotely sensitive to any cultural values. Some of your so-called kitty party friends are the very image of vulgarity."

Their fight was over nothing, meaningless, but it was powerful enough to destroy their mood and create a rift. It was like the thin end of the wedge that they had been totally unaware of. It did not take much time for Reeta and Vivek to turn their household into a battlefield. The moments of intimate privacy had become a painful experience.

"Any physical communication with you is now an ordeal for me," Reeta told Vivek bluntly one day.

"I abhor it, too. Only my lesser instincts occasionally compel me to perform it," Vivek replied.

Reeta retorted with equal bitterness, "You're just a baboon in a rut. Having to put up with you disgusts me to the core! You're a boor, but, in the eyes of ignorant outsiders, you're the very image of perfection and elegance. What a farce!"

Vivek laughed cruelly and said, "You can't make any man happy."

She looked hurt. "You've lost me only because you have never been interested in anyone but yourself. You're selfish. You only worry about issues that concern you. I must tell you, in absolute honesty, that you've got everything in life but, in spite of that, you're a loser. You've failed to win a woman."

Vivek did not say anything immediately. Then, after a long silence, he spoke, his voice calm and deep. "There was once a time when I used to harbor a secret desire in me. It was the desire to be seduced by a woman. You, on the other hand, have been a cold bitch. You're just a marble statue, devoid of warmth and feelings. Neither can you give joy to anyone, nor can you derive any pleasure in and from anyone's company!"

Reeta's face reflected her rage. "Pursuing your ambition has turned *you* into stone. There isn't any room in your life for others. Believe me, in your personal life, you're just a big zero. Men like you can never win a woman over." She stopped, glaring at him. Her eyes had now an insane look. "You're sure to be deprived of the finer things in life. I accept that your mind is well-equipped, but, in contrast, your heart is a vast, arid desert." She trailed off, muttering to herself absentmindedly.

It was after this outburst from her that Vivek began to feel shock at the realization that the things she had been saying in her anger were not totally untrue. "Maybe we'll think it all over and sort out our problems," he said in a conciliatory tone.

"That's no longer possible. It's over between us," she said indifferently.

"I'll look into the root of our problems," he promised vaguely. "We'll discover some way out."

She burst into humorless laughter before saying, "A fractured soul cannot be put into its original shape. We're poles apart!"

"Why are you being so difficult? I'm trying to give you a chance," he replied, trying to sound ethical and generous.

"You're an egomaniac. It shows in your choice of words. Never, ever forget that. Some women are very happy with the security of a house. I won't say 'home.' For me, 'home' is a big word! Anyway, I'm different. I look for equality in a relationship. Marital morality is an extraordinary concept. It's based on respect for each other. I don't think you know what that is! Maybe it's because of your childhood." said Reeta heatedly, as if in one breath.

Vivek was stumped. He knew she was not completely wrong. "Okay, that's your own opinion. I can't change it. I feel only time will sort things out and set them right between us," he said philosophically.

"I agree," she said.

"Reeta, I seriously think we need to spend some time together," he said a few weeks later, when the dust had settled. "Why don't you also give yourself a break for some time? You have a running business and people around to help you with things, so there is nothing to worry about."

"Sorry, Vivek, but I really can't. You are asking me at the wrong time. I have so much on my plate that I can't even take a break to breathe."

"But what about us, Reeta?"

"What about us? What is wrong with us that we should worry about?"

"You don't think there is anything wrong? You spend your time doing nothing but taking care of your business and that leaves very little time for us to spend together."

"Who are you to say all this, Vivek? I mean, I can't believe it! When I needed you the most around me, *you* were too busy setting up *your* business! I have spent entire nights crying in this house, waiting for you to come back and realize you had someone waiting for you at home. Those lonely days forced me to find recourse in my work and, now that I have found some balance here, you want me to give it up and just forget things?"

"I am not asking you to give it all up. I know you have gone through a lot, but I was working day and night for us, so that we could have a happy life."

"You were doing it for yourself and not for us, not for me. You had an ambition and you were working towards it, so do not try to hide your incompetence as a family man behind this veneer of doing things for us."

"What are you saying, Reeta?"

"The truth! You might not realize it, but I have lived a very empty life even with you around. Your presence is as good as your being absent from my life."

"I am asking you to take time off so that I can make up for all the lost time and we can revive everything we have lost."

"No, Vivek, not at the cost of my work. I have too much to take care of right now and can't afford to slip up. Anyway, I am tired and need sleep. See you tomorrow at breakfast. Good night."

***

One day, Vivek decided to surprise Reeta by visiting her in her office on his way back from work. When he arrived, Reeta's secretary told Vivek that someone had come to see Reeta and that she had gone to the coffee shop at the Taj with him. At first, Vivek thought of waiting for her, but, eager to meet her, he decided to go find her at the Taj.

The moment he entered the Taj, he saw a woman who resembled Reeta from behind. He went to the table she was seated at only to discover her chatting and laughing with Arjun, an old flame of hers and their common friend. At first, Vivek felt a little uncomfortable, wondering why Reeta would meet Arjun (in a coffee shop, that too) after so many years without informing him. He then gave her the benefit of doubt; maybe two friends were just meeting after a long time. However, the thought that they had been lovers in the past continued to disturb him. He decided to quietly leave the two of them undisturbed, go back home and wait for her to return and tell him about Arjun.

It was nine p.m. when Reeta finally reached home. Seeing Vivek waiting for her at their home bar, she was taken by surprise, as he usually got back after her. He asked Reeta to sit next to him, hoping she would want to tell him about Arjun. She sat and asked Vivek to make her a Bloody Mary. She told him about all the happenings of the day, but very conveniently avoided mentioning Arjun. Vivek did try to get the answer he wanted by asking her if she had gotten late because of a client meeting that day.

"Yes, I had a hectic day at work and a client had come to my office, so I got late discussing things with her. Anyway, I'm tired today, so I guess I'll call it a night," said Reeta.

Vivek asked her if she would like to have dinner with him, but she refused, saying she had had pizza in office and was not hungry. Her phone suddenly rang. Her face brightened up. Containing her happiness, she got up from the chair and rushed towards her room. Vivek could hear her speaking in whispers and giggling behind the closed door of the room.

He was left both confused and shocked by her behavior, confused because he not able to understand why Reeta would hide her meeting with Arjun from him and shocked because he could not digest the fact that she was lying to him. After a few drinks, he was too tired to think about it any further, and he, too, went off to sleep.

Coming home late became a norm with Reeta after this. Whenever he called on her cell, it would either be switched off or busy. Her office people would always tell him that she was either out on client meetings or had gone out to meet a friend. At home, too, she behaved strangely and did not take any interest in Vivek's life. Her only interest at home was her phone; she seemed to be constantly messaging someone with a look of sheer happiness on her face. Life was becoming increasingly difficult for Vivek. He, too, had started spending more time at work again, but this time he did not hear Reeta complain about anything. He knew that his marriage had failed miserably and that Reeta was seeing someone behind his back. He was convinced that it was Arjun. He had seen her with him on a few more occasions and, on his occasional visits to her office, had also seen bouquets sent to her by someone with the initials "A.S.," which obviously stood for Arjun Singh. What had transpired between the two in the past that led to their breakup, he did not know and had not even bothered to ask about, but what was happening between the two of them now was becoming a matter of concern for him. He finally decided to put an end to this game of cat-and-mouse and confront Reeta.

One day, when she came home late from work as usual, Vivek asked her to join him in the study. Reeta followed Vivek, but before he could say or ask her anything, she declared, "I'm pregnant."

For a second, Vivek wonder if he had heard her incorrectly. "What! What did you say, Reeta?"

"I'm pregnant, Vivek, and I'm not too excited about it," she said, sounding annoyed.

Ignoring her comments, he burst into a smile and, jumping with joy, said, "I don't believe it! I'm going to be a father! I mean, this is the best news you could have ever given me! Thank you so much, Reeta! I love you!"

"I don't think you heard me correctly, Vivek. I said I'm not amused by the news. In fact, I found out about it two weeks ago but, at that point, I didn't know how to convey it to you as I was not convinced about it myself."

"It's okay, darling. It happens. I know it must be big news for you to digest, so I can understand your feeling the way you do. Girls at your age do feel this way. But don't worry, with time it'll sink in and you'll also feel happy about it."

"No, Vivek, I don't think so. I don't think I'm ready for motherhood yet. My career is going great guns and there is so much more I want to do. With this baby, it will all come to a halt. I can't afford to give it all up just because I'm pregnant. Babies can wait, but not my career."

Vivek had briefly forgotten about what he had brought Reeta into his study to discuss. The news of the arrival of the baby had given him so much happiness that his memory had been wiped out momentarily. But the harshness in Reeta's words and her direct proclamation about not wanting the baby brought it all back. He started to piece the puzzle together. He knew why she did not want the baby. It was not for her career, but for Arjun that she did not want the baby. Having a baby would mean not meeting Arjun anymore. He suddenly started to feel sick in his stomach, as if someone had punched him so hard that his entire system was shaken. He was so angry that he wanted to slap Reeta then and there. But, controlling his anger and his urge to confront her about Arjun, he said, "Reeta, try and understand what I'm saying. You can work despite the baby. A baby can never be the reason for putting a stop to your career. In fact, the baby will be your stress-buster, and I'm here to help you at every step. I'll take care of the baby too."

"*You* will be here to help and support me, Vivek? *You?* Where were you all these years? How can you even think I'd trust you? You weren't there when I wanted you to love me and care for me. Your entire focus was on your business, so much so that you forgot I even existed. It was at that time that my work provided me solace. I got so deeply involved in it just to escape from the depths of my loneliness. Now, the very thought of not continuing with it gives me nightmares. I don't want this child right now and I have decided against it. I'll get it aborted."

"Stop it, Reeta! Have you lost it?" Vivek shouted back. "I know the reason behind your decision! Is it not Arjun who has compelled you to take this step?"

Reeta looked at him with shocked eyes.

He continued, "You thought I'd never get to know about it and you two would continue with your secret affair behind my back? I'm not a fool, Reeta. All along, I have known that you were meeting Arjun secretly. I have myself seen you two enjoying each other's company a couple of times but kept quiet, thinking you would soon realize your mistake and come back to me. But I guess I was wrong. Look what your audacity to find love outside this marriage has brought you to. You're even ready to abort our child! Don't you feel even slightly bad about it? Aren't you ashamed of saying it?"

"Stop it, Vivek! Had there been any marriage left between the two of us, I wouldn't have felt the need for Arjun's company. And, for your information, I'm not having an affair with Arjun. Yes, I do meet him and go out with him, but there is nothing beyond that. He gives me the attention I always craved from you. If being with him makes me happy, what's wrong with that? It doesn't amount to infidelity. He is my friend and that's it."

"Okay, if that's the case, why didn't you tell me about him? Why did you continue to meet him behind my back?" Vivek asked, bewildered.

"Because I knew you wouldn't like it. I know you have never liked Arjun because he was my ex. But you can never understand the fact that two former lovers can be friends, too, and remain just that. You can never achieve something like that in your life, as you have never been able to strike up a friendship with anyone, not even your own parents or sister. For you, there is nothing called love. You just live by the emotion of practicality, with your work as your only companion. I wish I had seen this side of yours before getting married to you, and trust me, if I had, I would never have agreed to the marriage."

Vivek, by now feeling bad about what he had said to Reeta, moved closer to her to hold her in his arms and wipe her tears. But Reeta was too hurt to let him do that. She said, "Vivek, you'll never understand the stress I have gone through all these years. I had a dream for us and you ruined it all for me. My work is my only support now and I won't let go of it. I don't wish to fall into the trap of your words anymore. Having lived with you for so many years, I have realized that it isn't in you to love anyone. As for Arjun, you can think whatever you wish to about him, but it will not change anything between us."

After making her point clear, Reeta stormed out of the study, leaving a distraught and totally heartbroken Vivek behind. Not knowing what to do with himself, he just collapsed on the chair and sat there, stunned, for hours. At around two a.m., when he came to, he got up to go look for Reeta and try to beg her for forgiveness. But he realized it was a bit too late, as she had already left for her parents' home. She had written him a note explaining everything.

Days passed and, when he did not hear from Reeta, he decided to go over to his in-laws' place and meet her. Vivek had become a sorry figure. He had stopped going to work. His dishevelled look shocked Reeta, but she decided to stay calm.

Reeta's mother's face brightened on seeing Vivek, but his slovenly appearance disturbed her.

"Is something wrong with you, son?" she asked with genuine concern.

"No no, just a bit tired. I have been working all night," said Vivek casually.

"You must take proper rest," she said.

"I will," Vivek promised.

"Have you come to take Reeta with you?"

He looked at Reeta. There was a look of alarm in her eyes. Noticing it, Vivek said, "She can spend some more time here if she wishes so. She can come with me otherwise," he said, slowly and with pauses. "Without her, my house seems like a desert!"

His words assured and delighted the old woman. "Love is like that," she said. "I'm really delighted to see you together. Now, you talk, and I'll send tea for both of you."

When she had left the room, turning towards Reeta, a sad and dejected Vivek said, "Reeta, I know what I did was wrong, but I think you should come back home with me so that we can have a discussion about the baby."

Reeta softly replied, "Vivek, I don't wish to discuss anything with you and there is nothing you can convince me of. And as for the baby, I have already aborted it."

Her words felt like a thousand swords digging into his chest. He felt as if someone had poured hot lava on him and his skin had burnt to ashes. Agonized beyond words, he said, "How could you do that to our child, Reeta? Please tell me this isn't true. Please!"

"No, Vivek, it's the truth. I'd told you earlier, too, that I wasn't ready for a child yet and thought that this was the best thing to do for myself. So I did it."

"'Myself?' Reeta, only you? Since when has this marriage become just about 'myself?' Where has 'us' gone?"

"Please, Vivek, I do not want to start this conversation again. I have already told you that this marriage is over from my side. I have no feelings, nothing, left for you. There was never really any 'us' in this marriage. It was just you and you. I have had enough of your eccentric life and now I want a life of my own, where I have reasons to be happy and also someone to share my space with."

"Please, Reeta, try and understand. I love you a lot. Please do not talk like this."

"Vivek, if you are done, I would like to put an end to this conversation."

Vivek had nothing more to say to her. He knew it was the end of everything. The baby had meant the entire world to him. He had promised himself that, with his child, he would be nothing like his own parents. He knew he had it in him to love his baby, nurture it, let it live the way it wanted and not the way some generations of rules and regulations demanded. His chance to redeem himself one last time through his baby had been snatched away from him. He had had dreams of living the childhood and life of his fantasies through his baby and, in the heat of the moment, that chance had been taken away from him by his wife. He saw the death of the dream, of the life he had thought he would be able to live. Life held no meaning for him anymore. His work and money meant nothing. He stood motionless for a few minutes.

Reeta said to him, "Please don't talk about this in front of my parents. They know nothing about it."

Vivek was too shocked to hear anything at this point. He got up and left. He did not know whether he met or saw anyone from his in-laws' family on his way out of the house. He left his car parked in front of their bungalow and started walking. Flashes from his childhood were playing out in front of his eyes. His parents' strictness, his trying to maintain distance from them…it all started to prefigure in his mind and he began feeling dizzy. What Reeta had told him had shaken him and traumatized him beyond words.

He walked and walked. He did not want to go back home, as he felt that the loneliness of the house would kill him. There was no question of going to his mother and there was no Reeta, a crutch he had found for a while and had now lost. He was all alone. He wanted to run from everything. Escaping the tragedy of life seemed like the only resort, but he did not know where to go. Suddenly, the honking of a car jolted him back to the present.

The driver of the car shouted at him, "Are you deaf? Can't you hear my honking? Why are you walking in the middle of the road?"

Vivek became aware of how stupidly he was behaving and apologized to the man behind the wheel. He turned back to see he had brought the traffic at an intersection to a halt, as he was standing right in the middle of a busy road. He looked around, apologized to no one in particular and ran from the scene. He went back to Reeta's house to pick up his car and drove back home.

He spent the night tossing and turning in bed. Demons from the past continued to haunt him and his sleep was distressing. He saw flashes from his past that disturbed him. His life had been a saga of failed relations, be it with his father, mother, sister, other relatives or, most recently, Reeta. He felt as if he was not doing anything right. The fact that so many people were blaming him at various stages in life and telling him there was something wrong with him only reinforced his belief that no relationship would last for too long in his life. He was entirely consumed by this thought and it caused his stress levels to rise.

He thought of Rammo. He fondly remembered his sweetest moments with her. Her expansive bosom was a cradle of security. In those memories was the sweetness of life. He wished he could visit her again. She was a mother to him then. She was the very embodiment of care and tenderness. He was overpowered by a sudden and intense nostalgia.

Derelict

He got up, walked to the bar in his home and made himself a potent drink of whiskey, and then another, and then one more. His lonely little party went on until the early hours of the morning. Having drowned himself in alcohol, he finally managed to sleep and woke up at around three in the afternoon.

The realization suddenly dawned on him that going away, leaving everything behind, was the only way to escape the memories of this house, this city and the people associated with his life. On the spur of the moment, without a thought about anyone, he took a small suitcase out of his closet, packed a few clothes and books and left. He informed his mother that he was going to a meditation retreat for a few days to a remote town in the north-east and might not be able to contact her regularly. He told her to take care of herself and that he would meet her once he was back from the trip. He did not bother to inform Reeta, as he did not think she would be interested. Moreover, he himself did not feel inclined to tell her about his life anymore. He just walked out of the house, called for a taxi and asked the driver to take him to the Old Delhi railway station, unsure of why he said station and where exactly he intended to go. He just decided to let his instincts plan things for him.

Upon reaching the station, he made a pact with himself—he would not look at the final destination printed on the ticket. He asked a stranger to buy him a ticket on any available train without telling him the name of the train or where was it heading; just the coach number and his seat number. He thanked the stranger, paid him a tip of Rs. 1,000 for helping him and started for the platform. The station was filthy, filled with people of all classes and backgrounds. For a moment, Vivek did think about reconsidering his decision, but the thought of going back to his life gave him a shudder. He thought it better to plunge into the unknown than remain in the known and suffer. The stranger had told him the train was already at platform seven. He reached the platform, boarded the train and sat down on the berth allotted in his name. Sitting across from him was a man, his wife and their two teenage children…

A New Motive in Life

Vivek did not realize how much time he actually wasted thinking about the past. Induced by something someone might have said or done, he would feel himself being transported at arbitrary moments to incidents in the life he had left behind. It was a bad habit and Vivek knew he had to get rid of it soon if he truly wanted to move ahead in life. Those memories could well be casting a horrible spell on his future and, now that he had come so far away from everything and was trying hard to change things about himself, his habit of living in the past had to go.

One particular phone call helped.

While he at his favorite tea shop one morning, he thought of Reeta and decided to call her up. If his time in Divi with Paresh and his family had taught him anything, it was to not run away from difficult situations.

He went to an internet cafe and made the call. He was surprised he still remembered her number.

"Hello?" Her voice sounded cheerful.

"Hi," he said with hesitation.

Her attitude immediately changed. She knew who it was, of course. "Where have you been?"

"Somewhere."

"You didn't think it necessary to tell me?"

"Reeta, I needed time off. I'm sure you know how it must have felt."

"I know, Vivek. But escaping is not the answer. When will you learn that? Anyway, I want a divorce and I need an address to send the papers to," Reeta said with a sigh.

"Of course. I'll send it to you today." Vivek knew his future was being built for him.

"And Vivek? Tell your partners at work where you are, what your plans are. This is the business into which you put so much of your energy and time. It demands responsibility and respect. So do your friends," said Reeta.

"Yes, of course. Thank you. Thank you, Reeta, for everything," Vivek said before hanging up. For some reason, the words "responsibility," "respect" and "friends" conjured Paresh's face in his mind. But he knew that he had to sort out the past before moving on.

It was time to get a smartphone.

Thinking about Paresh through this haze of thoughts about the past, the future, friends and responsibilities, Vivek's mind suddenly lit up. What if Paresh's business could grow beyond Divi and Ankleshwar and reach the masses? What if he could convert this simple and modest *samosa* business into a million-dollar enterprise? By now, he had tasted the *samosas* many times and he was sure they were the best by far in the country. It was time to introduce this simple man, Paresh, with his simple values but extraordinary talent, to the world and make everyone sit up and take notice of him. He had been languishing in the dark for too long. He had to step up and claim his due.

Vivek knew that people in the railway stations, where Paresh did his best business, were crazy about the *samosas* and the chutney. Those customers would get the *samosas* packed in large quantities and carry them home. The whole day long, if there was one thing that was flying off the shelves at the station, it was "Matru ka *samosa*." "Matru ka *samosa*" was like a celebrity in its own right; people bought platform tickets to be able to eat it! At Paresh's shop, people queued up to buy them first in the evenings. After six p.m., it was difficult to even get any leftovers. And, yet, this man Paresh remained unaffected by it all. For him, the praise that he got was the biggest reward.

He was not greedy and certainly not egoistic. He knew he had a talent but could not conceive of misusing it. He stayed true to his commitment, which was to supply high-quality *samosas*. He had dedicated his entire life to this one thing and he did not want much in return.

To Vivek, this was one great quality of Paresh's that motivated him to help the pure, uncomplicated soul. He did not want to corrupt Paresh by making him fall prey to the politics of the big, bad business world. All he wanted was recognition for Paresh and to set an example through him, that no matter which section of society one was from, if one had the right inclination, grit, determination to succeed and the will to remain true to one's intent, the sky was the limit.

Vivek's mind was buzzing with ideas. He decided to lay out his plan for Paresh's future before him that night after dinner and was hoping that they would then start marching towards achieving those goals. He was once again excited about something in life. He felt as if he had found something to live for and was determined to go for it. At last, he was coming back into his own and was feeling charged up about taking on this new challenge in his life.

A Planner at Work

At night, when Paresh got back home, Vivek announced to him that he had something really important to discuss with him after dinner. Paresh asked him what it was, but Vivek refused to let on. All he said was, "Be prepared, your life is about to take a big turn."

Paresh found the spring in Vivek's step amusing. He assumed something good had finally happened in Vivek's life. The fellow seemed to have acquired a new vigor, and Paresh was happy to see him relaxed and enthusiastic about something. He told his wife to make arrangements for him to sleep in Vivek's room.

After a very heavy dinner of *bajra chapati* loaded with pure *desi* ghee, a dish of green peas and potatoes, yellow lentils, curd and salad followed by a glass of milk, they all proceeded to their respective rooms.

Not able to contain his excitement anymore, Vivek told Paresh, "Paresh, are you done with your dinner? Can we go to my room and talk about the thing I had mentioned now?"

Paresh nodded his head in agreement and they both went upstairs to Vivek's room. "*Haan ji*, tell me the good news. Has something really important and auspicious happened in your life today? Have you decided to go back home?"

Paresh's last sentence caused a sigh of disappointment to escape Vivek's mouth. His mood suddenly went from that of a happy man to that of a dejected man. "Go back home? Is this not home for me? I thought, Paresh, that I had become part of the family. I felt pretty much at home here. I didn't even once think that you so desperately wanted me to go back to my own place. If that is the case, I shall leave tomorrow morning, as early as possible."

"What are you saying, *babuji*!? Not even once have I thought of you as an outsider. To me, you *are* family and I'm more than happy to have you here as an important part of this household. I didn't mean to say that you should go back. My only concern was that your family would be waiting for you and might be worried about you. I don't know why you left them behind and came here and nor do I intend to know, but I said it only because you seemed so happy. Please forgive me if I have hurt you in any way. My intentions were pure. Believe me."

Believing he had hurt Vivek's sentiments so much that the young man would actually leave, Paresh started touching Vivek's feet in order to beg his forgiveness. Vivek grabbed Paresh's hands and said, "What are you doing, Paresh? Please stop it! Okay, I get your point and understand what you meant. I mistook your meaning. Never mind. Let's end this topic here and get on to discussing what we have come here for."

"Are you sure you're alright, *babuji*?" asked Paresh, still concerned.

"Yes, I am. Now, can I please tell you what I intended to?" asked Vivek.

"Of course, *babuji*."

"Let's make you rich and famous. I have a plan for you and I want to see you succeed. And to begin with, stop calling me '*babuji.*' This is not how you're to address me from this point onwards. My name is Vivek. Please call me that."

Worried that Vivek hadn't recovered from the shock of their minor misunderstanding, Paresh said, "*Babuji,* I really am sorry for what I said, but you don't have to pull my leg over it. How can I ever address you by your name? Your stature is much higher than mine. I wouldn't feel comfortable calling you by your first name."

"Paresh, I'm not joking. I'm very serious. Please call me by my name, I'm okay with it. But, more importantly, I have laid out a plan for your business to grow beyond this small town and the few stations that it is restricted to right now," Vivek added.

"But, *babuji*…I mean, Vivek…*ji*…no, I can't. I'll call you *babuji* only! I'm a very small man with limited money and resources. I'm happy where I am right now and don't think I'll be able to bear the burden of more risk, as far as money is concerned. Whatever I make on a daily basis, a major part of it goes into running the business and the rest goes into savings for the future. I don't think this is a very good idea," Paresh said.

"Listen, Paresh, I know what I'm talking about. Okay, call me whatever you want to, but listen to me carefully, please. Only after calculating all the permutations and combinations relating to how you can benefit from this plan and all that is required for it am I proposing it to you. Look, I'm a man with a good business sense. I know how to run a business. You have a rare talent and it would be a crime to keep it restricted to a small area. I think the world has a right to taste your *samosas*. And a talent like yours needs the right platform to grow. Had you been someone average, trust me, I would have never dared to suggest this to you. I don't believe in massaging the egos of people just for the heck of it. I have seen something great in you, something that goes beyond your talent. Your integrity is your greatest asset and I want you to be truly successful. I know that, given the right direction, exposure and opportunity, you can do wonders. And, most importantly, I owe you something, so don't say no to this."

"Thank you, *babuji*, for your kind words, but I don't think I'm worthy of all that you are saying. Yes, like everyone else, I also dream of growing big, but I'm not greedy for fame and money. Not, at least, to the extent where I'd start building dream castles. I know where my limit ends and so have stretched my capacities to that point only."

Hearing the simplicity with which Paresh explained his situation, Vivek once again felt deeply for him. What a humble and down-to-earth man Paresh really was. Had it been someone else in his place, he would have grabbed the offer and opportunity without a blink. But here was this man, neither arrogant nor greedy despite his talent and the wonders it could do for him.

Vivek said, "Paresh, you aren't alone in this business. It is the livelihood of your family, too. For your wife and kids and your sister, it is that one source of money on which their life and future depends. Think about them. Even they have dreams and desires to fulfill. If your growing can give them the freedom to fulfill their wishes, what is the harm in that? Okay, think of it from this point of view. If you grow big, you'll require a bigger shop and more people to help you out. The people whom you appoint will definitely be from this town. So, in a way, you will provide them employment and help them earn for their families. And with your popularity increasing, more and more people will get to know about Divi and its U.S.P. You never know what kinds of opportunities this place might offer to bigger business houses when they learn of it. It could be a game-changer for the people of this town. Try and think big, Paresh. With one move, you can change the lives of many people."

For a moment, Paresh seemed to have been convinced. But once the ground reality of his not having enough money to put at risk hit him again, his world came crashing down. He said, "*Babuji*, your idea almost convinced me and, trust me, I'd be more than happy to be able to do anything for this town and its people—they too are part of my big family— but the fact remains that I don't have any spare money and I don't want to put the money I have saved into such plans. We are simple and somewhat poor people, *babuji*. For us, whatever money we have is enough to keep us going for the rest of our lives. Like our status in society, our dreams and desires are also small; so small that they can be fulfilled with whatever money we have. As long as we have a roof over our heads and get three square meals a day, we're happy. Making it big and driving fancy cars and travelling abroad are things we aren't meant for. Even if we desire those things, we learn the hard way that reality works differently or get lost trying to attain even the basic necessities. I know, *babuji*, that whatever you have planned for me is for my good, but I don't think it'll do me any wonders. To earn money, one needs to have money and the ground reality is that I have none to spare. I'm content with the pace my business is growing at and, even if it doesn't expand, I have no regrets. I, too, have ambitions to reach out to as many people in the country as possible with my product, but I know that destiny and money have a big role to play in anyone becoming rich and, as for me, right now I'm not in a position to afford such a lavish dream."

The argument between the two went on until the wee hours of the morning. Vivek felt a compelling need to make Paresh consent to his plans so that he could get started with the entire process, but Paresh was hell-bent on not agreeing to anything.

Coming from the kind of background he came from, it was hard for Paresh to believe that an ordinary *samosa* maker could build a well-known and established business. All his life, he had seen his grandparents and parents struggle to earn one meal a day. He himself had grown up in extreme poverty and so he was satisfied with whatever he had been able to make of himself. Trying to make it big could also lead to failure and he was too scared of losing everything he had accumulated. His shop was his life and making *samosas* was all he had ever known. If this shop was taken away from him, he would be left jobless and even homeless. He did not wish to be a failure in the eyes of his kids and so kept on refusing all the help Vivek offered him. He grew tired of listening to Vivek and also realized that he wouldn't be able to reach his shop on time the next morning if their discussion went on any longer.

He finally said, "*Babuji*, I think it's too late now to continue this discussion. Let's pick this up again tomorrow. For now, I am quite sleepy so I think we should retire."

Even though Vivek wasn't in the mood to give up yet, he knew that he would have to keep Paresh in good spirits if he really wanted him to say yes, so he agreed. Bidding each other good night, both of them retired. Since Paresh was very tired, he went into a deep slumber the moment he closed his eyes. The funny thing about Paresh that Vivek did not know was that, while the *samosa* maker slept, his internal organs went into overdrive at night. His nose busily experimented with nasal sounds and his stomach grumbled. His high-pitched snoring kept Vivek up all night, battling the trauma of being caught in a situation where his only companions were the sounds coming from various parts of Paresh's body. At one point, Vivek thought he would not be able to survive the onslaught and might give up in the middle. He even thought of waking Paresh up and asking him to go sleep in his room downstairs. But, unable to find the words that would serve as an excuse for his decision to ask Paresh to get out of the room at such an ungodly hour, Vivek gave up the idea, gave in to his situation and started counting the minutes and hours left before sunrise.

The next morning, when Paresh got up at six, he found the room empty. He stepped out onto the roof to find Vivek inhaling from a small glass bottle containing a yellowish liquid. He jokingly said to him, "*Arre, babuji*, what are you smelling early in the morning? Are you fine? Hope it isn't some sort of morning sickness?"

For Vivek, the torment he had had to endure all night was nothing less than that sort of sickness. By dawn, he could not take it any longer and had rushed out of the room.

"*Babuji*! You look sick! Didn't you have a peaceful night?" Paresh asked, very concerned.

Vivek laughed. "It was a very musical night for me. But I'm quite collected all the same."

Vivek knew he would have to coax his way up to get Paresh's consent. He would have to try pushing a little harder. Once Paresh agreed, everything else would start falling in place.

Meanwhile, to tackle Paresh's stomach, Vivek decided to use homeopathy as his armor. Since childhood, he had been educated in the benefits of homeopathy by his grandfather, the official doctor at home. Even though he was not a trained doctor; reading extensively on the subject had made him a doctor minus the official degree. Anyone who fell sick would be medicated by Vivek's grandfather instead of an actual doctor. This interest of his grandfather's had been infused into Vivek, too, and even he, in his spare time, liked reading about homeopathy. So, when the need arose, he decided to go to the market and fetch Paresh some medicines that would help ease his stomach and provide him some relief from his flatulence. After much searching and asking around in town, he stumbled across a dilapidated shop that sold homeopathy medicines. Vivek asked the shopkeeper to make him small packets each of Carbo Vege, Pulsatilla and Nux Vomica in the potency of 30. Holding his armory close to his heart, Vivek went back home and waited for Paresh to return.

Rushing through his dinner, Vivek asked Paresh to follow the same routine as that of the previous night, as he wanted to jump back into the discussion. He also told Paresh that he had something to give him as a digestive aid after dinner. When Paresh reached his room, the first thing Vivek asked him to do was to gulp down small doses of the medicines. When Paresh asked him what they were for, not wanting to sound rude, he said it was only to help him sleep better as he felt Paresh had not been comfortable the previous night. Without questioning him any further, Paresh took the medicine. Vivek felt relieved knowing that he would be able to enjoy sound sleep that night. The two began conversing again.

"So, what have you thought about my plans, Paresh?" Vivek asked excitedly.

"*Babuji*, I already explained the entire situation to you last night. Why are you so bent on pursuing your plan?" asked Paresh, bewildered.

"Only because you deserve a better deal in life in my view. You, my dear friend, are endowed with real intelligence. Even at this point of time, I can visualize how you're going to make something big of your life. The possibilities are infinite."

"But where will all the money come from? Big ideas need big money in order to be executed," said Paresh.

"A loan! We'll go to your bank and apply for a loan. You don't have to worry about anything. I have charted out the entire course for you and—"

Before Vivek could finish, Paresh jumped out of his bed and screamed, "Loan! *Babuji*, what are you saying? Who will give a loan to a poor, nondescript and uneducated man like me?"

"Any bank would. In fact, banks are always on the lookout to invest in profit-making ventures or at least promising ideas. One just has to be able to convince them. And, for a small business like yours, which fortunately even enjoys market goodwill, they won't refuse."

"No, *babuji*, I don't think it's a very good idea. I'm a man with meagre means and nothing to wager in case I fail to pay them back. Involvement with banks is something I want to avoid. In fact, it's one major reason I never went to a bank looking for money when I wanted to start my business. Asking relatives and friends for money is an easier option, as one doesn't have to worry about what would happen if one were not able to pay them back at the designated time. You can always beg relatives and friends to give you more time and, in most cases, they do soften up, but with these big banks, there is never a hope of mercy. They can take away my money, my shop, my house and whatever little I have if I falter on even one of their payments. *Babuji*, I'm a very simple man, so let me remain that. I don't wish to get myself embroiled in any of these complex matters."

After a brief silence, Vivek said, "Paresh, I totally understand where all this is coming from. But trust me, I know these things inside out—it's not what you think it is. No one will take away your shop or house. Banks are not monsters. They're a stepping stone to your future success. The more help you seek from them, the better it will be for your business. In any case, you don't have to worry about bank formalities, all that I'll handle. You just sign the papers I ask you to. I hope you can trust me with that much at least."

"What are you saying, *babuji*. I have no doubts whatsoever about you. I completely trust you and will entrust everything of my own to you," said Paresh.

A smile on both their faces sealed the deal between the two. But, before sleeping, Paresh asked Vivek, "*Babuji*, by the way, how much are you going to apply for?"

"Five crores."

Paresh almost fell out of his bed. "Five crores! *Babuji*, I don't even know how many zeroes there are in a crore and you're saying we will apply for a loan of that amount! My entire life's savings don't amount to even a fraction of that amount. Even if I wager away every last penny that I have ever owned, along with this house and all my savings deposits and gold and silver, I don't think I'll ever be able to come close to even an iota of that amount. Please, *babuji*, forgive me, but I don't think I'll be able to go ahead with this plan of yours. I know you're doing it all for my good, but I don't want any generosity from you that could endanger the prospects of my family. Thank you very much, but I seriously don't want to be a party to this ambitious plan of yours."

Realizing he was back to square one, Vivek once again started. "Listen to me very carefully, Paresh. I have thought deeply about this plan and am certainly not shooting in the dark. To begin with, we will have to upgrade your shop and buy all the fitments that will be necessary to meet increased demand. A sizeable amount of capital will go into all that. Then, of course, money will be required to make your packaging look more attractive. Branding your product needs a great amount of work and, for you to be able to reach out to a bigger market and audience, you'll require a lot of capital. The loan that we're applying for isn't that big an amount. For you to hit the right markets and grow with a bang, all of it will be required. It was only after I had worked out the cost of everything that I reached this figure. Trust me, there isn't an extra penny that I have quoted."

"Still, *babuji*, I have a feeling that when things happen too rapidly they lead to disasters and I'm definitely not geared to face that."

"Okay, Paresh, if that is the case then I'll become your bank guarantor," Vivek said confidently.

"Bank…what?" a confused Paresh asked.

"Well, the guarantor is the person who provides a sort of security on behalf of the borrower. That is, in case the borrower fails to repay the loan amount or other dues to the bank, the guarantor pays; in this case, if something were to go wrong with your business, god forbid, and you were unable to pay back the loan amount, they'd get hold of me and not you. So, whatever capital assets I would have declared as a security against the amount borrowed would be taken away from me. Simple. Now, good night. We have a long day tomorrow."

"What are you saying, *babuji*? I can't let that happen to you! You're such a noble and helpful man. I can't make you pay the price on my behalf. It's no fault of yours if my business doesn't work, so why should they punish you? No, I won't let anything of this sort happen to you."

"Don't be so dramatic, Paresh. Nothing of that sort is going to happen. You need to start trusting my instinct. And besides, I'm not so generous that I would bet that big an amount without being sure of it. So, just forget everything now and go to sleep. I want to get up refreshed and relaxed tomorrow so that I can put my brain to good use," Vivek said, still confident, and went to sleep.

The night turned out to be good for both Vivek and Paresh. Paresh started believing in Vivek. Although not fully convinced about the entire plan, the dream of being able to provide his family with a better lifestyle nevertheless impressed him. He spent the entire night thinking about it. On the other hand, the biggest relief for Vivek was that it was an odorless night. He did not have to spend it tossing and turning. They got up the next morning totally refreshed. Vivek was proud of his achievements as a homebred homeopathy genius and decided to advise Paresh to take the dose every day.

Paresh, meanwhile, felt a change taking over him. He was happy that perhaps his life would take a turn for the better now and soon his fortune would be on the upswing. Although he was still unsure about whether the plan would really take shape the way Vivek had proposed, he was happy with the dreams he had had at night about his changing fortunes.

They greeted each other with smiles upon waking up. Vivek asked Paresh if he had his identification documents and all the other required papers ready. He took Paresh with him to the town market and got a set of passport size photographs made. Then he searched for his own papers, too, and put them all in order.

He inquired on the phone about the banks in town and learned that the nearest Mid-Scale Enterprises branch was 20 minutes from Paresh's house. They took a bus to the outskirts of the town with all the papers in tow. Before boarding the bus, on Paresh's request, they went to the local temple to seek the blessings of Lord Shiva and the local deity of the town. Paresh told Vivek that, because they were going to take such a big step in life, seeking the blessings of the gods was a must. Vivek, though an atheist, did not contest Paresh's idea and agreed readily. He did not wish to upset Paresh at that point in time for fear of another volte-face. Dressed in a crisp white shirt and grey cotton trousers, which he wore only on special occasions like weddings or family get-togethers, Paresh felt every bit like the businessman Vivek wanted him to be. Both lost in their own thoughts, they left for the bank.

A Meeting with an Old Friend

At the entrance of the bank, Paresh, feeling nervous, said to Vivek in a tremulous voice, "*Babuji*, are you sure you want to go ahead with the plan? I feel we should think about it once again. I'm still not convinced it's a very good idea."

"Now, Paresh, please don't start again. I have told you a thousand times that you don't have to be so nervous. Get your body language right, because if anyone senses here that we aren't sure about our work, they might not clear our loan. I don't want you to be the reason for anything going wrong. I have worked with an international bank in the past and, for my own business, I have dealt with these kinds of people many times. So trust me when I tell you it isn't that big a deal. It's a very easy and hassle-free process. Just stop behaving as if you are about to try climbing the Everest." With these words, Vivek confidently marched into the bank. Paresh followed him in like a puppy who had just been scolded for being naughty.

Vivek asked the person at the cash counter for directions to the manager's room. The cashier told him that their boss was in a meeting and would get free in an hour. He pointed to a sofa next to the door and asked them to make themselves comfortable there. Vivek and Paresh went to it and sat down. While Vivek once again busied himself with the papers, ascertaining that everything was in order, Paresh looked around and, for the first time in his life, observed every counter of the bank and tried to understand how its day-to-day business was carried on.

He realized that there was so much cash involved in the bank's everyday operations that he could live his entire life on the amount that must have been present inside the bank on that one day. The visit to the bank proved to be an eye-opener for him. To date, he had visited banks only to deposit the money he had saved in the two accounts he had opened: one to fund his children's education and the other for the marriage of his daughter. What went on behind the scenes was a mystery to him. Today, on gaining an insight, he felt his wealth of knowledge had increased marginally and he would love to bring Rajesh here someday to make him understand the workings of a bank. He felt glad to have come to the bank and thanked Vivek for it.

A little over an hour had passed and Vivek was now getting restless. He went up to the same cashier and asked him when the manager was expected to get free. The cashier told him that he had no clue as he did not keep a log of his manger's meetings.

The way the cashier replied irritated Vivek and he shot back, "Do you get paid to be rude to your clients?"

A battle of words ensued and, for a while, the workings of the bank came to a halt. Everyone's attention was turned towards Vivek and the cashier and the heated exchange of words between them. Two other employees of the bank and Paresh intervened to calm the flared nerves and it was only with them stepping in that things came under control. Vivek went back to the sofa while the cashier got back to his work.

After some time, Paresh said, "Are you all right, *babuji*? Should I get you a glass of water?"

"No, thank you, Paresh and I'm sorry for what happened. It's just that laxity in people often gets on my nerves. I find it really difficult to digest such an attitude. I should probably just let them be."

Paresh, meanwhile, felt that the fight was a bad omen. When things had started on such a note, only God knew what would transpire ahead. He started to chant the Gayatri Mantra to calm himself. This was the biggest step he had ever taken and, every time he thought about the money and all that was at stake, his blood pressure shot up. Since Vivek was a veteran at such dealings, he was obviously taking it as he would any other workday in his life, but, for Paresh, it was a major and significant event and he wanted it to be perfect. After an hour and 45 minutes, Vivek saw the door of the DGM's room open and someone come out. He got up and walked towards the room. A man, most likely the peon, was sitting outside the room and blocked Vivek's way at the entrance.

"What do you want, *sahib*?" he asked.

"I want to see your DGM," Vivek replied.

"Regarding what?" the peon asked.

"Regarding a loan. Now can you please stop interviewing me so I can meet him?" Vivek said arrogantly.

"Well, you need to have a prior appointment to be able to meet him. DGM *sahib* doesn't meet anyone without an appointment and I have been strictly told not to send anyone inside who doesn't have one. Sorry, *sahib*, get an appointment first and only then will I be able to let you inside his cabin."

Vivek was again on the verge of losing his temper, but he swallowed his pride so as not to create another scene in public and to save Paresh and himself from any further public humiliation and embarrassment. He asked the peon where he could make the appointment.

The peon pointed to the desk of the office secretary, who was sitting at the end of the row leading up to the exit door.

Vivek gingerly walked to the secretary and placed a request for the appointment. The secretary told him that it would not be possible for him to fix up a meeting for that day, but if they came the following day they would be able to meet the DGM. Vivek requested the secretary to somehow squeeze in a meeting for that day itself as they had come from far away, but the secretary refused. Disappointed and frustrated, Vivek returned to Paresh and told him everything.

While they both were contemplating their next move, a female voice interrupted them. "Excuse me, can I help you?"

Vivek turned around to see an attractive woman in her late twenties with a voice as sweet as honey and eyes as beautiful as those of a deer addressing him.

"I have been observing you two for quite some time. You seem upset about something," she said. "Is there anything I can help you with? I'm Divya Seth and I'm the accounts head here."

For a while, Vivek was so mesmerized by her eyes and voice that he just kept staring at her. He had never seen a face as pleasant as hers before. After all that he had gone through in the past few months, her voice and looks hit him like a breath of fresh air.

Confused about why the gentleman was staring at her and saying nothing, the woman again asked, "Sir, can I help you with anything?"

Vivek came back to his senses and began struggling hard to find the correct words to respond with. "Yes, I wanted to meet your DGM, so if you could arrange a meeting with him it would be good."

"Hmmm, okay, let me see what I can do for you. Give me a minute, let me go and speak with the DGM." The woman vanished into the manager's room and reappeared minutes later. "Okay, your work is done. Manager Sir has agreed to see you for precisely 15 minutes despite his very tight schedule. So hurry up and make your point," she happily informed Paresh and Vivek.

Before rushing towards the DGM's room, Vivek thanked the lady and told her, "I don't know what you said to him that made him agree to meet us, but whatever it is, all I can do is thank you. A man's destiny is about to be changed forever and you've played a great role in that. By the way, I'm Vivek Kapoor, just in case you are interested in knowing my name."

"Okay, Mr. Kapoor, you can thank me later, because, if you're late, my boss may not want to meet you."

Vivek hastened towards the DGM's room. The name plate on the door read Siva Nagarajan. *Sounds familiar*, he thought. Instructing Paresh to stick to only the mandatory "yes" and "no" answers, he knocked on the door.

"May I come in?" he asked.

When he entered the room, the first thing that struck him was how modestly it was done up, with nothing to grab anyone's attention. There was a framed photograph of Mahatma Gandhi hanging on the wall right behind a man who had his head buried in piles of paper. Adjacent to that on the wall were images of Krishna and Kuber. *The man is of a religious bent of mind*, thought Vivek. Without disturbing the man, he and Paresh entered the room and sat down across the table from him.

"Would you like tea or coffee or anything?"

To Vivek, the voice sounded too familiar, but he did not pay much heed to the thought. He said tea would be just fine. The manager buzzed someone on the intercom and placed a request for two cups of tea and one cup of coffee. *How soft-spoken and humble this chap is*, Vivek thought. All the while, the man had not raised his head even once to look at Vivek and Paresh or make eye contact with them. He was busy reading and signing papers and it was very clear he did not want to be disturbed. A few seconds after they had taken their seats, the DGM lifted his left hand and signaled towards no one in particular, as if asking them to begin with their story.

Vivek said, "We're here to apply for a loan."

"What kind of loan and for how much?" the man asked.

"Well, it's for an SME and the amount is five crores. I have all the papers and applications ready with me and I have prepared the necessary project report and a presentation as well."

The man gestured again with his hand, this time to ask Vivek to stop. He then said, "There are close to about 20 people who come down every day from far-off places to meet me. They all have the same agenda, that is, to secure a loan of x amount, and they all give me numerous presentations, but only one out of those 20 gets lucky. In short, I have heard enough of these pitches, so if you have anything interesting to say, then speak up, otherwise don't waste your and my time."

Vivek was taken aback with the man's brutal frankness. Realizing it was time for him to wear the hat of a shrewd businessman, Vivek said, "I know you must get a lot of visitors every day with all sorts of requests, but I'm not here to request anything. All I'm saying is that if you aren't interested in my plan, I won't hesitate for a moment to leave this room and visit some other bank. I know my business idea is brilliant and will surely work and my success will be your loss and some other bank's gain. So, before dismissing my case, it is you more than I who needs to do a rethink."

Now it was the DGM's turn to get his head out of the papers and see who this confident man was. As soon as he lifted his head, both Siva and Vivek cried in shocked unison, "I don't believe it!"

Paresh was thoroughly confused and wondering what exactly was going on in the room. The two gentlemen got up to greet each other with a hug. Unable to contain the excitement of meeting an old college friend after years, Vivek began speaking with great enthusiasm.

"Where have you been all these years? What an incredible surprise to see you here, man! I mean, I still can't believe it's you!"

Siva said with the same warmth, "Same here! I would have never imagined meeting you again after so long in a place like this, where you have come to ask for a loan. Gosh! It's been years, *yaar*."

For the next 15–20 minutes, both of them got caught up with each other. Recollections from their days in college cropped up every two minutes and filled the room with laughter.

When Paresh felt that the two of them had gone on with their chitchat for long enough, he butted in. "*Babuji*, we were here to talk about something important. Remember, that lady outside told us that we have only 15 minutes with him."

"Oh yes, Paresh, thanks for reminding me. By the way, Siva, this is Paresh. The loan that I was talking about is in fact for him. I want to help him expand his Indian snack business and for that I need your help and guidance."

"Oh, I see. Show me his papers and let me study his case first. These days, the banks are getting very tough with their rules, so a thorough screening of the papers and proposal is a must. I cannot commit to anything without going through them, but can assure you that, if all of them are in order, there is no one who can refuse you the loan. Just leave your papers here with me and come see me the day after tomorrow. I'll do a thorough analysis by then and will be able to give you a better and clearer picture."

All three of them then had another round of coffee and the talk veered back to their college days and beyond.

Siva asked Vivek what he was doing in that small Gujarati town. Vivek said, "There are times when one doesn't plan things, but they just happen. This town and Paresh are among the few things in my life that have happened not by my design but by destiny's. I'm here now trying to help Paresh grow his business and my current focus in life is only that."

Siva did not probe any further. Their exchange continued and what was supposed to be a 15-minute meeting ended up stretching to a good two hours. The two then took leave of Siva and headed home.

On their way out of Siva's cabin, Vivek bumped into Divya once again. She asked him if he had been able to get his work done. Vivek told her that Siva turned out to be an old friend, so he was confident of getting the loan. He also thanked her once again for being so helpful and mentioned that he would meet her again when he came back. The two then took each other's leave and Vivek and Paresh walked out of the bank.

A Step Towards a Dream

Back home, Vivek's entire evening was spent thinking about Divya. After the meeting with Siva, his confidence about the loan increased manifold. He was sure it would get approved. He had never had any doubts about his own capabilities, but with Siva coming on board, his belief was cemented. A different kind of matter now clouded his mind. He had never heard a voice as sweet as Divya's. And those eyes…they had a hypnotic, beautiful quality. Vivek was hooked.

He was desperate to go back to the bank, speak with her again and look into her eyes. He had never felt this way before. When he had met Reeta for the first time, he had been hesitant and not too comfortable opening up to girls. But this time, when he met Divya, he realized it was a different feeling. He wanted to speak to her. He wanted to hear her out, know more about her and spend more time with her. He was excited about going back to the bank because that would mean another opportunity to see her and talk to her, even if it was only for a brief moment. Although he did not know what about her was proving so attractive to him, he wanted the feeling to continue as it gave him happiness.

Lost in thoughts of her, he did not realize that night had descended. He was not hungry enough to go down and check if dinner was ready or curious enough to talk to Paresh about any plans either. He had become a different person and everyone seemed to have noticed, but they left him alone, assuming that he wanted some time off from everything.

Rajesh brought Vivek's dinner to his room. Vivek, lost in his thoughts, didn't notice Rajesh coming in and going out. After a while, when hunger pangs finally disturbed him, he saw a plate of food on the table next to his bed. He picked up the plate and gobbled down his dinner. He was not remotely concerned about how the plate had reached there. All he wanted was to finish eating so that he could go to sleep and dream about Divya. It was mindboggling, how the brief meeting with her had impacted him. He wondered what it would be like to know her from up close. He didn't know when he fell asleep, but it was the soundest sleep he had had in recent times.

He continued to move around as if in a daze the next morning. He did not bother about breakfast either and didn't leave his room until late in the day. Fearing for Vivek's health, Paresh went to his room to check on him.

"*Babuji*, I hope you are fine?" asked Paresh, quite concerned.

"Yes, I'm absolutely fine! What's wrong?" Vivek replied.

"No, nothing. It's just that, since the time you have come back from the bank, you have been very quiet and have also lost your appetite. *Babuji*, there is nothing to be so tense about. I know this loan is bothering you. But why worry so much about it? That bank manager is a friend of yours. He seems to be a nice man and I'm sure he'll help us, like he said. Please don't worry. Come down and have something to eat."

Vivek was in no mood to contest anything Paresh said. He quietly followed Paresh downstairs, finished off his breakfast of *aloo paratha* with curd and went out for a walk. He spent the whole day dreaming about Divya. It dawned upon him around evening that he had been behaving like a lovestruck idiot the whole day and that he must snap out of this mood now, but the thought of finally seeing her the next day struck him then and he was again transported back into that same mood.

He spent the entire night getting up at intervals, checking the time and impatiently waiting for dawn to break. The moment the clock struck six, he hurriedly jumped out of his bed, bathed and took a sky-blue shirt and khaki trousers out of his suitcase. He polished his shoes to the point that he could almost see the reflection of his own face in it. All ready and smelling of musk, he went down and asked Paresh to hurry up with his chores as he did not wish to be late to the bank. Although their meeting was scheduled for noon, Vivek told Paresh that, since it took almost 45 minutes to reach their destination by bus, he did not want to risk missing the first bus. In fact, his real plan was to reach the bank by 10 so that he would get ample time to talk to Divya and get to know her.

They reached the bank at 10 sharp. The bank had just opened for the day and its employees were trickling in. The two of them went inside and made themselves comfortable on the sofa. The peon jumped up from his seat and went to fetch water the moment he spotted them. Most of the employees had realized during their last visit that Vivek and Paresh were important people, as the manager had never entertained anyone for so long and with so much laughter in his cabin. The employees did not want to end up in their DGM's bad books, so behaved very courteously with the VIPs. The cashier with whom Vivek had had an altercation of sorts the last time kept to his work without bothering about Vivek's presence in the room.

But Vivek was oblivious to all that was happening around him. All he wanted to know was when Divya would walk into the office. With his eyes fixed on the door, his face dropped every time someone else walked in through the door. It was 45 minutes past 10 when Vivek got up to walk to the peon.

"What time does Divya madam usually come to office?" he asked the peon.

The peon got up from the chair and said, "*Sahib*, she is usually in office by 10. I don't know why she is late today. Maybe she is on leave. I don't know yet."

Disappointed, Vivek went back to the sofa and sat down. After another 10 minutes, he noticed a woman walking into the room talking on her mobile phone. It was Divya. The mere glimpse of her lit up Vivek's face. His smile came back and he began to blush as if someone had paid him a compliment. She walked past without even noticing him and headed straight to her cabin, Vivek's eyes following her every movement. He had hoped that she would notice him at least once and give him a cue to exchange words with her. But, to his misfortune, nothing of that kind happened. Still, he was happy about having seeing her. It was 11:15 and he was again getting impatient. All that while, Paresh had been sitting next to him and patiently observing activities in the bank, but he had seen the change in Vivek, too. He wasn't surprised when Vivek asked him, "What do you think of Divya?"

"Divya?" Paresh inquired, feigning ignorance.

"The woman who helped arrange our meeting with Siva the day before. The bank's accounts head," Vivek told him.

"Oh yes, that lady. She was very nice. In fact, I'd like to thank her myself for her kindness. What a pure soul she was to help us! But why are you asking about her, *babuji?*"

"No reason. In fact, I share your sentiments and was also thinking that we should thank her personally for her kind gesture," Vivek said quickly.

Not wanting to prod Paresh further lest they start discussing things that were only meant to be fodder for his own mind, Vivek decided to end the discussion there. Suddenly, the door of her cabin opened and she emerged from it, looking regal in a crisp and cottony yellow-and-white *salwar kameez.*

What a pristine beauty she is, thought Vivek. His heart skipped a beat at the sight of her. He suddenly got up and walked up to the photocopier machine where she was waiting to collect printouts.

"Hi!" Vivek said. Divya turned around to find Vivek standing right behind her.

"Oh, hi. So we meet again," she replied in her honey-dipped voice.

Thankfully, she is not pretending to have forgotten meeting me, thought Vivek.

"How have you been?" asked Vivek.

"I'm good. How are you and your friend?" She looked towards Paresh.

"We're doing well, too. In fact, a while ago we were talking about you. Had it not been for your generosity, we wouldn't have been able to meet Siva. And he turned out to be an old classmate. So basically, it was due to your divine intervention that I was able to get my work done and also meet an old lost friend," Vivek said to her, somewhat flirtatiously. It was uncharacteristic of him and took even him by surprise, but there was no turning back now.

"Oh no, please don't embarrass me like this. It was nothing. It was just that I could see how hassled you and your friend were feeling, so I thought that if I could help you in any manner, I should. It was just that and nothing else."

"Still, I want to thank you for everything." Vivek was very excited to talk to her, so much so that he forgot it was almost time for the meeting.

Paresh walked up to Vivek and Divya and interrupted their conversation, saying, "It's 12. We are supposed to go meet Manager *sahib*."

At that point, Vivek gave Paresh a sharp and agitated look. Obviously, he was not amused with this interference and almost felt like asking Paresh to get lost. But he did not wish to lose his temper in front of everyone, especially before Divya, so he just said, "Yes, Paresh, I know it's time for the meeting. You go sit and I'll join you in five minutes."

Paresh went back to the sofa. *What a spoilsport Paresh is being*, Vivek thought. He hurriedly told Divya that he would catch up with her later, took her leave and signaled Paresh to join him while making his way to Siva's cabin.

Vivek knocked on Siva's door. This time, the peon did not stop him. A voice from inside said, "Come in, please."

They entered. After exchanging the usual greetings, all three settled down.

"I read your proposal, Vivek, and had a word about it with my seniors, too," said Siva. "The good news is that the bank is happy to fund your idea. In fact, my seniors were very pleased with the reports and case studies you presented with your application. I think they made your presentation more insightful and detailed. But my question to you is, will Paresh—don't mind my saying this—with his modest understanding of business, will he be able to deliver? I mean, it's you who have proposed to be a guarantor here, so God forbid, if something untoward happens, it's you who will suffer the most."

After taking into account Siva's concern and pausing to think about how to respond, Vivek said, "I know what you're pointing out as a concern here, but trust me, Siva, this man has a talent and all I'm doing is helping to give him a platform through which he can do something better and bigger in life. I know he isn't from the big bad world of business and doesn't understand the economics behind it the way we do, but his integrity and determination compensate for everything. His innocence is his advantage and gives me the confidence that he'll succeed. As far as my risk as a guarantor is concerned, I'm least bothered.

"I, too, have built up a business of my own from scratch in the past. So I know how to go about it. I'm not mad for money. Had that been the case, I wouldn't have left my own business behind and gotten myself into something like this.

I'm using the fixed deposit money I got as part of my share in my father's business against the loan. So, even if I lost that money, it would not harm me much. I'm not saying losing that big an amount wouldn't be a setback, but I'm confident of my ability and, to back me up, I have a man as talented as Paresh. I do not for even a moment doubt the venture's chances of success. Besides, I'm here to help him establish what already exists. He already enjoys the goodwill of his ardent customers, which I'll explore a bit further. Everything will be sorted out."

"Well, if you feel this way then I have no doubt that you'll be able to make good this move," said Siva. "I have always known you to be a confident guy, so I wouldn't be surprised if I saw you two on the cover of Forbes magazine someday. All the best to both of you. I hope the next time we meet, you will have grown bigger."

"Siva, we will keep meeting now that we're in the same town," said Vivek. "Meeting you after so many years has brought back happy memories of our days in college, a part of life I definitely want to keep in touch with." The three of them then proceeded to discuss the remaining paperwork that Vivek and Paresh would be required to fill out before they could get the loan. A good two hours later, and much relieved, they ventured out of Siva's cabin. Vivek again spotted Divya standing near the photocopier and walked up to her.

"I have to give you the good news."

Caught unawares, Divya was a bit startled, but she managed to smile at Vivek and excitedly asked, "Really! What is it?"

"Well, we got our loan approved and now can happily get on with the work," Vivek said.

"Wonderful news. Congrats!" Divya wished them both all the best.

Testing his luck, Vivek said, "Divya, since you have played a major role in us bagging this loan, I have to compensate you in some manner. How about a coffee? My treat."

Even though Divya was not the kind to accept such offers from strangers, she readily accepted Vivek's offer. Vivek then took her number and told her that he would call her up in a day or two and to decide upon a place to meet. The two then bid each other goodbye.

Vivek and Paresh left the bank starry-eyed. Paresh, because he had just taken his first step into the world of business, the world he had imagined that only people with power and money could run; and Vivek, because he had won the first round of the battle for Paresh and, as a reward for it, gotten the chance to meet a girl as wonderful as Divya. They decided to take home some sweets for the kids as it was a happy occasion and they wanted to have a small family party.

Vivek spent the next few days running from one place to another, getting things in order. He sourced people who could supply the best raw material. He even spread the word about openings for people who would want to work as helpers and assistants in Paresh's shop. He went scouting for a bigger place where all the necessary equipment would fit and for a warehouse. Arrangements for a makeshift cold storage were also planned so that perishable food products could be stored in it. During this time, Vivek shuttled between different towns and cities like Delhi and Mumbai. Whenever he was home in Divi, he would spend his time surfing the net to learn about the latest machinery being used in the food industry. He would make Paresh sit with him and discuss what they could do for the business.

Paresh had heard a lot about the power of the Internet, but had never had seen firsthand how it worked. He could not believe that, sitting in Divi, he could undertake a virtual tour of the world. His excitement knew no bounds when he was given a virtual tour of his future factory, through which he saw exactly what it would look like and how the machinery would be used. He soon began thinking of the Internet and the laptop as nothing less than manifestations of God.

Vivek had taught Paresh how to use a laptop. The Internet had initially bewildered Paresh, but he soon began taking great interest in it.

"Paresh, I think you are enjoying yourself now," Vivek noted.

"Yes, *babuji*, that's right," said Paresh, flashing a smile at Vivek. "I feel I have understood it completely now."

"I don't believe you, Paresh. Show me something to back up your claim," said Vivek to tease his friend.

"Okay, *babuji*—look at the ease with which I operate it!" Paresh said and pressed a button.

Suddenly, a porn site popped up. Images of Sunny Leone and Mia Khalifa appeared on the screen. Paresh was extremely shocked and embarrassed. Vivek burst into laughter.

"What's that, Paresh?" he asked, faking shock and surprise.

"I don't know how these ladies appeared...I...I...am really sorry...I didn't intend it..." said Paresh, stuttering.

Putting an assuring hand on Paresh's shoulder, Vivek said, "Take it easy, Paresh. After some time, you'll become adept at handling these unexpected situations."

Paresh was completely at sea after the exposure to those provocative photos of nude men and women indulging in sexual activities. He lost his mental balance and was in a limbo state for most of the day, refusing to speak with anyone. He thought he had sinned and the fear of being caught and branded a sexual predator wrecked him. It was only later in the day, when he saw Vivek working at the laptop with no traces of what they had viewed during the day anywhere, that he experienced relief. He even asked Vivek if it was possible that, when someone logged off the Internet, the last viewed image was frozen in place so that the next time someone logged in, the same image would be viewed by that person, too. It was only when Vivek answered in the negative that he felt happy again; he had made up his mind to never touch the laptop again otherwise and had even made plans to visit the holy city of Haridwar to wash away his sin.

Vivek, meanwhile, was back in his element. He had once again renewed his contacts with old friends and people he knew in the business. He had called up his two friends and partners to inform them that he was not to be expected to rejoin work anytime soon but would still be available on the phone in case they needed any assistance, help or guidance from him.

After many recces and much deliberation, he called up an old engineer friend of his and invited him to Divi to advise him about the suitability of constructing a plant on the land he was planning to buy for the factory. It was only when his friend gave him the nod that Vivek bought the land and initiated the process of plant construction. Hell-bent on getting the best support in terms of equipment, technology and people, Vivek decided to leave no stone unturned. He was busy putting everything in place while Paresh continued to operate from his old shop. Looking at the speed with which everything was being planned worried Paresh a bit as he still thought all of it was a dream. For him, the way money was flowing in, machinery being tested, TQM processes being put in place and strategies being drawn in consultation with various people was a bit staggering.

He had been the sole decision-maker in his work, but now, with experts stepping in and with Vivek backing him big time, he realized what he had lacked until now. Earlier, he was of the opinion that large enterprises were run by a sole operator and that person was the only one who called the shots. But the exposure he was being subjected to opened his eyes to a much bigger picture. He realized that a group of evolved minds have to come together to run any organization. It is a conglomeration of people who came together to run it, an institute based on one man's vision but run by several minds, who are aligned with that vision. He understood that, even if he was not alive tomorrow, the vision would continue to live through the work of others. His business would survive, as those who would now be associated with it as equity holders or stakeholders would see to it that it fortified itself and moved in the right direction.

Vivek was also instrumental in making Paresh understand that the inflow of money was to now come from people who would be interested in staking their money on taking the idea forward. What had started as a small idea would now be fueled by many to enable it to take a bigger shape. It took him time to understand the dynamics behind the running of a big business establishment, but since Paresh was a quick learner, he eventually did become adept at those things.

Meanwhile, making use of every contact he had, Vivek procured the phone numbers of canteen owners at MNCs and hospitals. Although his plan was to start a separate chain called Matru ka Samosa and go big, this was the level he had decided to start at. Once he sealed the deal with a couple of clients, he came back to Paresh and told him that now was the time for him to get into action. Overnight, Paresh went from being a *samosa* maker operating from a small shop to being a big business owner operating from a huge shop that had all the latest kitchen fitments.

Paresh was at first intimidated seeing so many tools inside the shop and almost did a U-turn. Scared, he said to Vivek, "*Babuji*, I have never seen so many tools in my life. All my life, I have made *samosas* using just a knife to cut potatoes and a flat surface to knead the dough and roll it into the required shape. I don't know what these things are and fear that I'll ruin them all."

Vivek laughed and said, "Don't you worry, Paresh, I have people coming from Delhi to help you understand the working of each of these things and they'll also help you with your work. I have also spoken with a few local guys who will help with the delivery process. I know that these things are new for you. But using these tools will push your productivity up several notches. If you were previously able to roll out 5,000 *samosas* in a day, using this equipment you will easily be able to make around 50,000." He paused, groping for words that would convey to Paresh the significance of these things with greater effectiveness. "My dear Paresh," he said, his tone conveying the seriousness he felt, "it's only our first step towards becoming a giant global eatery chain. In the coming times, our activities will multiply geometrically."

Paresh's eyes almost popped out of their sockets on hearing Vivek's words. He had never been able to roll out *samosas* in such huge quantities and now, with these machines, he would be able to make more money. He suddenly fell at the feet of Vivek and said, "*Babuji*, you have come into my life like some God. I don't know how to ever thank you. I owe you for life and don't think I will ever be able to repay you, not even with my life."

Vivek bent down to lift Paresh up. He said to him, "Paresh, I have told you repeatedly, I am doing nothing for you. You have the talent, not me. I'm just helping you put it to better use. You don't have to thank me for anything. And if you ever try touching my feet again, believe you me, I'll leave everything and go away."

"No, *babuji*, please don't ever say that. Okay, if you don't like all this, I won't do it, but please don't ever talk about going away again."

To lighten the mood, Vivek teasingly said to Paresh, "A future business honcho shouldn't be found begging to an ordinary person like me."

They both laughed and Paresh, with folded hands, again thanked Vivek and continued to look at his new workplace with awe. This was the first of his baby steps into the business.

Cupid's Arrow Once More

In a couple of years, the small shop of *samosas* had grown into a big factory equipped with every facility that was required to churn out thousands of fresh *samosas* accompanied by delicious chutney.

Although Paresh was no longer running the kitchen, he continued to oversee the cooking procedures himself on a day-to-day basis. With time, his involvement and understanding of the business had evolved and he had proposed to Vivek that they should pitch to the government the idea of having special railway wagons carry their supplies to other cities, since it would generate more employment opportunities in town and benefit the economy of the country. Vivek did his own research on the proposal and came up with commendable insights into how the idea could be pitched to the railway ministry.

He then used his contacts in the ministry to take the deal forward. The best minds were again engaged to work on a brilliant idea that would convince the government. The advantage with Vivek was that he was a highly effective mediator. He knew the people who mattered in political circles and how to get things done. He would run from pillar to post, drawing up strategies and dismissing ideas that he thought were trash. He put his analytic skills to good use, chalking out plans, presenting them to the people in power and motivating his team to push the proposal forward. The team that he had built comprised a group of highly motivated, educated and skilled professionals, selected by him after much research and deliberation. He was satisfied with the progress they had made and he was now sure that, with them around, the work was sure to reach new heights of success soon.

While all this was happening, one day, Vivek realized that it had been a long time since he had spoken to his mother. He decided to call her and try to repair the fissures that had been created in their relationship over the years. Now that he had found a new beginning, he wanted to see everything from a fresh perspective. To him, it was almost like starting life afresh; he wanted no bitterness or baggage from the past to cling to him.

"How are you, Ma?" he asked her on the phone in a very emotional tone.

"How are *you* and where have you been all this while?" she replied, her voice full of concern.

"I told you I was going to a meditation retreat. There were certain unanswered questions whose answers I longed to seek. I was on a trip to discover them."

"Did you find them?"

"I found more than answers, mother. I think I'm a much calmer and more sorted person now. I'd have never thought of coming to the place where I stay now, but I'm grateful to my destiny for having brought me here and given me a motive to live. I'm now living a new and contented life, mom. I have freed myself of all my past demons and feel as if I have been born again."

"That's great, *beta*. I have missed you all my life...the son you could have been...but even if I find him now, I'll be happy."

Vivek did not take kindly to this. He felt as if she were pinning the blame on him. Maybe his mother had become too detached from the world now to really understand what he was talking about. Ever since her retirement from the active social world, he and Reeta had been the only people with whom she would converse at length, so her bitterness, whatever it was about, was acceptable to him. He knew she was too egoistical to take it all upon herself. He decided to accept her words calmly. Maybe that was the change in himself that he was referring to.

"Yes, Ma, I know what you mean. But what can we say about life and the games it plays. You never had the time to talk to me and the distance between us just grew. Now that we're trying to come close, a lot has to be addressed and we still need to give each other space and time to understand the stages of our respective lives that we are at. I promise not to hurt you, but you have to accept who I am calmly, too. That is a request from your son and I hope you will consider it."

The two continued to talk for another 15–20 minutes. He inquired about Neha and her husband and about many other things. He signed off by saying he would come see her in Shimla soon and that she should take care of herself. The conversation left Vivek feeling weighed down with emotions. He did not feel like going home, so he started going through the contacts on his phone, wondering whom he could speak to next. Suddenly, his eyes stopped at a number he had almost forgotten. It was Divya's. In the excitement of putting Paresh's business in place, Vivek had almost forgotten about her. It'd been almost two years and he was not sure she would even recognize him or want to talk to him. He mustered up the courage to dial her number, but disconnected after just one ring. After some hesitation, he thought of giving it a second try and dialed the number again.

A sweet voice on the other side of the phone said, "Hello!"

Vivek's heart skipped a beat and he began to relax.

"Hi, is this Divya?" asked Vivek.

"Yes. Who is this?"

"Divya, it's me, Vivek."

"Oh, hi Vivek! How are you? I was wondering where you had vanished."

Relieved that she did remember him and had also been thinking about him all this while, he regained his confidence.

He said, "Well, after our loan was approved, we got busy setting everything up. I know I should have called you, but it was all so very hectic that I just didn't get the time."

"It's okay, Vivek, I can understand. So tell me, is everything settled now? Do you need any sort of help from me?"

"No, absolutely not. I just wanted to ask if my coffee offer was still on. I mean, would you still like to go out for a cup of coffee with me?"

"Of course. Tell me when and where you would like to meet."

"I'll meet you outside your office tomorrow evening. Let's then decide where to go then. Is that okay with you?"

"Sure. I'll see you around five, then. Bye!"

Vivek was happy and smitten again. The thought of meeting Divya once again, after so long, got him excited and charged up his mood.

The next evening, Vivek starting getting ready well in advance of his date with Divya. He wanted to be well turned out for the evening and to impress Divya at every level, so he took out a crisp white shirt and a pair of jeans from his bag. Looking dapper in his clothes, Vivek left at 4:30. Parking his car outside the bank, Vivek called her up.

"You've arrived?" Divya asked, picking up.

"Yes, I'm outside the bank waiting for you."

"Okay. Give me five minutes, I'll meet you outside."

Five minutes later, Divya emerged from the bank. Wearing a pink cotton sari with a white blouse, she looked like a divine spirit to Vivek. He was seeing her almost after two years and she still looked the same. In fact, the years had only added to her beauty—she had become more charming with the passage of time.

"Hi, Divya!" said Vivek, his eyes glowing with happiness.

"Hi! How have you been?" she asked, smiling.

"You look beautiful!"

"Really!" She brushed past the words with a laugh.

"I mean, I have been doing well. Slightly busy, but yeah, good," Vivek said, trying hard to cover up for his kneejerk reaction.

"I know a place where they serve amazing coffee," Divya said "The Army Club in Ankleshwar is absolutely marvelous. We can sit beside the swimming pool and have coffee."

"Army Club? They will not allow us in. I mean, we don't belong to the army."

"My father does. This club was opened by some of the ex-servicemen. I am a member. Okay, let's not waste any more time. We'll resume our chat at the club."

Vivek, unable to digest so much stimuli, started the car. They headed for the club. Once inside, they sat at a poolside table and continued their chat.

"You like it here?" said Divya, her limpid, large eyes watching him.

"Yes. In fact, I think this place is better than those coffee shops mushrooming by the dozen in town. I don't think you can find this ambience anywhere else."

"Yes, having spent my entire life in these army cantonments, I have come to love army clubs. They provide you with the best facilities and also give you the kind of privacy you want. Who could otherwise think of swimming around in a bikini in a place like Ankleshwar?" she added.

"True. So, you *are* an army girl. Interesting. When I first saw you at the bank I could tell you were no small town girl. You looked out of place in that office, with all your grace and smartness. I should have known then that it was a product of your army background. The pretty face, the refined manners."

"Just the manners part, if you say so—I have my genes to thank for my face," she retorted. They broke into laughter.

Vivek found out everything he could about Divya. Since the day he had first seen her, he had been curious to know about her. The more he was getting to know her, the more attracted he was. She was a well-read, well-travelled and intelligent girl. She had grown up in an atmosphere that gave her the freedom to be whatever she wanted to. She lived in a small town now, but her level of exposure was greater than most city kids. Having been the head of the debating society in her school, she was a smooth talker. Her knowledge about various subjects, ranging from politics to literature to sports, impressed Vivek and he felt he could go on listening to her for hours.

After having answered many of Vivek's questions, Divya asked Vivek to tell her everything about himself and how he had come to live in the small town of Divi. At first, Vivek tried hard to dodge all the questions, but he realized that hiding information would not do him any good. If he wished to talk to her and get to know her better, he would have to tell her everything about himself—his troubled childhood, his reclusive college days, his meeting Reeta, his marriage, his abrupt decision to leave everything behind and his chance meeting with Paresh.

Fearing she might not want to meet him ever again if she found out how somber his life had been until then, he tried to cut out major parts about his past. But once he started, he was unable to control himself. With her, he felt as if he were speaking to a confidante, a friend he had longed for all his life. Suddenly, it dawned on him that, the more he spoke about his past, the lighter he felt. He knew that he was at risk of losing this friend, too, but he found himself unable to stop.

After having spoken for almost two hours non-stop, he suddenly stopped. Realizing that he had been the only one speaking all this while and fearing that Divya might not actually have been interested in his entire life story, he said apologetically, "I'm so sorry. I didn't mean to talk about all this and bore you. I had asked you out for coffee so that we could spend some time together and here I've been the only one talking—that too about nonsensical things. I'm very sorry to have spoiled your evening. I think we should leave now."

Embarrassed with himself, Vivek got up. Divya said firmly, "Wait, Vivek! Please don't leave. It's okay. Believe me, I don't feel bad about it at all. In fact, I'm very happy that you have shared so much about your life with me, so much that you otherwise would not have shared with anyone else in your very first meeting. I would say you are a very brave man and very truthful, too, as you did not hide anything about your past from me. I don't know what shape our friendship will take in the future, but at least we won't have anything to hide from each other."

Divya's words gave Vivek the assurance that he was not wrong about her. She did not only have a beautiful face—her soul was equally beautiful. Their conversation continued until around nine, when Divya told Vivek that she would have to leave, as it was getting late for her. Vivek offered to drop her home and she readily agreed. After dropping her off, Vivek reached home in a very happy mood.

Sensing that his *babuji* had had a very pleasant evening, Paresh teased him, "So, *babuji*, how did it go? Seems like you had lots of fun. The blush on your face is giving away the story of your evening."

He really was blushing. Divya had him completely in her spell. He was lost in thoughts of her and he knew that day would mark yet another beginning in his life. A beginning full of love and affection.

A Loony Lover

In the silence of the night, Vivek kept thinking about Divya. She was the very embodiment of sweetness and tenderness. The way she had patiently listened to his life story and had not, even once, felt overwhelmed by it had him completely smitten. Her assurance that she would still like to keep in touch and continue the friendship made him feel secure. He wanted to think about other things, but he could not. The time he had spent with her had his psyche in its grip. In fact, he did not want to forget the evening at all. *It must be the beginning of love*, he thought. He smiled at his own obsession.

After he fell asleep, he began dreaming. In the dream, he was leisurely walking about in a place he could not identify. He had read about such places only in fairy tales. The manicured garden, fresh flowers, clear blue sky, birds chirping, juicy fruits hanging from trees…it was like the Garden of Eden. There was a golden tree right in the middle of the garden that caught his attention. Fountains gushed multi-colored water. He was enthralled.

"Vivek!" someone called out.

"Who is it?"

"Look back!"

He looked back. "Divya!" he shouted, incredulous.

She smiled. "Were you thinking about me?" She flashed a seductive smile at him.

He looked at her longingly. "How can I think about anything else?" he asked.

"You're a loony lover," she said, rather coquettishly.

He took her hands in his. They were soft and warm. They excited him. A strange sensation ran through his body and drowned him in its sweetness. He began reciting a poem.

"I want to merge my breath with yours,

And forget the whole world around me now.

By losing my own self into yours,

I'd come by love's infinite variety."

"Vivek!" she said sweetly.

"I'm not just a sentimental lover," he said softly.

"I know that," she assured him.

He drew her closer to him. Her breath was intoxicating. The musk she was exuding had some primitive quality. It smelled sweeter than the flowers in the garden. His arms went around her body. She did not resist his advances. Rather, she seemed to be enjoying them and even reciprocated the gesture. He looked down and met her gaze. They looked into each other's eyes for a long time. There was a strange smile on her lips. Observing her closely, he was delighted to see the same longing in her eyes that he felt. She seemed to him the most beautiful woman on the planet in those moments. His hand moved up and down her exquisite body. Her derriere was round and tight. Her tumescent nipples were pressing against his chest. He was overcome by intense longing. He bent down and thrust his lips upon hers. Their soft moistness honed his desire further. Feeling himself harden, he could not hold his passion back any longer. He wanted to possess her, own her, plunge into her depths.

"Divya!" he crooned in a low tone.

She looked up. "Yes?"

"Will you share your life with me?"

She burst into soft laughter. "A million times, my asinine, lustful lothario," she uttered flirtatiously.

They held each other tightly.

The dream ended. Divya melted into the air. Vivek woke up with a start.

A Brand is Born

A considerable amount of time had passed since Vivek had first come to Divi. Paresh had gone from being a small shopowner to an operator of a well-established business and was growing with each day. His dedication and focus were producing good results. In a span of a few years, he had learned how to use the new technologies with ease. Neelu no longer assisted him, as he had a considerable retinue of people working in the shop and helping him with everyday chores. He was happy that his wife was enjoying her time at home and with the children, doing things she had otherwise not been able to.

"Neelu, I am finally a happy man."

"Were you not happy earlier?"

"I was, but the fact that you don't have to toil hard gives me immense relief. I hated seeing you perform so much labor. But now, with God's grace, everything is going fine and I am happy to see you at home more often than at the shop."

"But I enjoyed it there with you. It was for our home and children that we were working. I did not regard it as hard labor."

"I know, Neelu, you are not the kind to complain. You would live the rest of your life bearing the burden of my troubles without saying a thing."

"That's because I love you. But I *am* upset about one thing."

"What is it, Neelu? If you want something, tell me and I will get it for you. A new *sari*? Jewelry? What is it?"

"No, those things are of no value to me. I am upset that I get to spend very little time with you. At least I would get to be around you when I was at the shop," Neelu said with a hint of disappointment in her voice.

"I know, but don't worry. I am still very much here and you can drop in whenever you feel like—not as a worker now, but as the owner of the place," Paresh said, laughing. Then a quiver entered his voice. "Neelu!" he whispered emotionally.

"Yes?"

"Get used to this exclusive, farmhouse way of life."

"I find that it leaves me somewhat unfulfilled. Maybe all this pomp and show isn't in my genes," Neelu said in a low tone.

He felt a sudden surge of love for her. Embracing her, he blurted out, "I have the best moments of my life only in your company, Neelu!"

She smiled with happiness, but said absent-mindedly, "I feel lonely at times. Even Rajesh is away now."

"Be proud of him, Neelu! Your son is now a student at Pittsburgh University. He has a great future ahead of him."

Paresh's home was finally being taken care of by the woman of the house. She would often drop in at the shop with lunch for both Paresh and Vivek. She was happy that her husband's business was growing at a rapid speed. The entire house had undergone a makeover and was now among the major attractions in the town. It was huge and beautiful and had the latest amenities and facilities. The interiors had been planned by Vivek and he had made sure that only the best quality material was used. He used the latest teaching aids. From air-conditioning to plasma televisions to DVD players and everyday household items like a food processor, microwave and induction cooker, to bathroom fittings like bathtubs and commode faucets, he had had all the things the kids had only seen in serials and movies installed. The kids had made it a point to show these exotic appliances and fixtures off to their friends. They had often come home after school with their friends and taken them around the house, knowing that these friends would go back and spread the word the next day. But the parents remained as humble as they had been when Vivek had first met them.

While serving food one day, Neelu told Vivek there was something new for dinner.

"What is it?" asked Vivek, smelling something divine.

"*Bhaiya*, nothing much. Just *dal bati churma*."

"Oh, sounds fabulous!"

It was as good as the aromas had promised.

"Where did you learn to cook so well, Neelu?"

"I have always been interested in cooking. My mother and grandmothers taught me their secrets," she said shyly.

"These are all awesome recipes and very well-prepared, too. Behind these four walls, you're cooking food that is often better than what we get in five star hotels."

"Oh, *bhaiya*, you're too kind. I enjoy all of this and it keeps me happy," said Neelu.

Vivek had found another example of the practical and humble choices of the people he now called his family. Paresh had absolutely none of the airs of a successful man. He still went to work on his cycle, as he said it kept him fit. Neelu still did all the household work on her own. She could easily have hired a maid, but she felt it would corrupt the essence of being a homemaker. Besides, she would have nothing else to do the entire day. She still had the same set of friends and would often go to the river banks in the evenings to chat with them.

Augmentation of money and resources had not changed them one bit and they still continued to be the grounded people they had always been. If success could not corrupt them, Vivek was sure nothing in the world could. He felt proud of having taken the huge risk he had for them. He believed they deserved it and he would continue to help them for as long as he could. All in all, the growth of the business had ushered in good times for the family and they had just one person to thank from the bottom of their hearts…Vivek.

Vivek, on the other hand, was actively taking care of the marketing. A good five years had passed since he had first met Paresh and now Paresh had become well-versed in handling things by himself. He would, every morning and evening, personally check the delivery boxes. He would supervise the cooking process himself to keep the quality under control. He would constantly be in touch with the delivery boys to ensure the deliveries were reaching the designated areas on time. He would personally see to the unloading of the raw material every morning to check for anomalies. Finances and accounts were solely managed by him. Matru ka Samosa was quickly gaining national recognition. Everywhere that it was being sold, Vivek would get reports that they flew off the shelves within a matter of a few hours. With more demand pouring in, the shop had to be expanded even more and more equipment and people brought in.

Vivek was a marketing genius. He designed a website for the brand and updated information about it in order to keep customers abreast of all developments. He wanted to bring them much closer to the process and the people behind it. He had many contacts in the media and was able to secure widespread coverage of the brand on various local and national TV channels and newspapers. Soon, Matru ka Samosa gained momentum and became a household name in Delhi, Mumbai, Punjab, Uttar Pradesh, Himachal Pradesh, Madhya Pradesh, Bihar, Rajasthan, Haryana and many other parts of the country. Apart from railway stations, the brand had also opened franchise outlets in various parts of the country and, every day, fresh supplies of *samosas* were being delivered to them. Soon, more Indian savories like *kachoris* and *pakoras* as well as sweets like *jalebis* and *gulab jamuns* were also added to the menu, each more delicious than the other. Every product became a hit with the masses as well as the classes.

With demand increasing, the time was ripe to export to the overseas markets. Soon, consignments were being sent to the U.S. and the U.K. NRIs quickly became huge fans of Matru ka Samosa. Never had Paresh imagined that his *samosas* had the potential to go international and he was happy that he was alive to see this happen.

Another Vision – From Divi to Olympic City

Now that things were going smoothly, Vivek worked with more vigor. He was a man with dreams and the wherewithal to make them come true. But something had stuck with him since he had come to Divi. During his walks in the narrow lanes, he had often noticed boys with exceptional athletic skills and wondered whether they really did have some innate talent. He began to invite them to a largish ground next to a pond and to play with them. Sometimes they played cricket, sometimes football, and sometimes they just ran or jumped or climbed trees. Slowly, a picture began to form in his mind. He could see these youngsters doing much better with training and he wanted to do something about it.

Very quickly, the number of boys coming to play increased manifold. Most had to wait for their turn to play or ended up scrambling about together on the ground, which had now become too small to hold everyone.

On his walks back home, Vivek's face would be flush with excitement and an energy he didn't remember ever feeling before. "This is what happiness must feel like," he would say to himself.

Days became weeks and weeks became months. Matru ka Samosa was had moved on from its baby steps with Paresh's knowhow and hard work and Vivek's vision;

meanwhile, Vivek's new dream began to take shape. He was soon trying to locate bigger spaces to play in and, sure enough, was granted access to the municipality ground, which was lying largely unused and had become a garbage dumping ground. Children now began coming in from every part of Divi to played with Vivek. With his keen sportsman's eye, he could see that there were many boys and girls who were exceptionally talented. He had not been able to pursue sports due to circumstances, but now he had the opportunity to get others to play.

After some digging on the internet for information about training raw athletes, he began to call children early in the morning for exercise. He was absolutely certain that the work in progress at both ends—*samosas* and athletics—would completely nullify all of the anguish he had experienced in his life. He thanked his stars for having boarded that train and having agreed to get down from it when asked.

Within a few months, his dream expanded. He wanted to train a 100 boys and girls for Olympic-level performance. The dream started becoming a reality. A big, different, new reality, just the way he had imagined. With the help of many of his friends and batchmates and consistent support from Divya, he tapped the right people and secured both direct and indirect help to give his dream concrete shape. His good intentions and hard work had become a topic of much conversation in the town and beyond.

Some businesspeople of the town agreed to sponsor a few big events and one corporate house that had a key office in town guaranteed nutritious food for the 100 boys and girls selected by Vivek for their potential to make it to the Olympics. This district administration had taken a keen interest in the project, too, and the District Collector had assured Vivek of help in finding more fields, hostels for the trainees and food and sports apparel. Reputed coaches had agreed to periodically visit and guide the trainees for just a nominal amount.

Vivek found himself thinking about the challenges ahead and his faith in the power of the new generation to overcome it. He had seen that power in the young boys and girls, felt their passion and energy. Together, they had already come a long way.

Olympian success needed Olympian preparation. The mind, body and spirit of the trainees had to be perfectly tuned to the rigorous demands of the job. Vivek hired expert physiologists to study their physiques and recommend customized exercises, diets and super-foods. He collected training videos that documented the phases of preparation that Olympic- and Asian Games medalists went through to surpass all odds and achieve glory. His boys and girls took inspiration from the videos to harness their hidden strengths and initiate the necessary transformations in themselves. Many of them started showing unthinkable improvements in their performance standards within a short span of time. The whole architecture of the build-up to the Olympics was working wonders in sculpting each athlete to bring out the best in himself or herself.

Reaching the playground one morning and seeing all the athletes busy practicing, Vivek started clapping and cheering them on. He suddenly called out, "Hey, boys and girls, just come here for a second. I have something to say to you. Come fast!" The sight of them converging around him made him feel proud. "Okay, listen, all of you. I want you to win over everyone around you with your disciplined conduct and sportsmanlike spirit. Understood?"

"Understood!"

Then, in a lighter vein, he said, "We will all have a great time. Don't worry, I'm not going to test you. We will just celebrate our 100 champions—you! As you all know, we are here to live a dream. My dream. Your dream. And the dream of a new India. This is our great Olympian dream." With an intense expression on his face, he asked, "Are you all ready? Are you ready to make it big in the Olympics?" Not getting a roaring response, he felt that the weight of the dream had become too heavy a burden on the shoulders of the young kids. They needed a pep talk. With a change of tone, he started again. "I know the job isn't easy. I know what it takes to become even a state or national champion and here we are talking of the Olympics! Maybe the prospect scares you." He paused and then asked, "Tell me, do you know who Pele is?"

"He is a great football champion," murmured someone in the audience.

"Correct. He is an all-time great, a legend. Do you know that he used to fear the ball and was scared to play at one point in his life? But he kept playing, because he knew the game would help him rise out of poverty one day. When he started playing, he used a rolled-up sock stuffed with old rags as a ball. Did you know that?" Pausing for a bit to let this sink in, Vivek continued, "Have you heard of Ronaldo? I'm sure some of you are fans of his?"

"Yes!" came the answer, this time a little louder.

"You must be aware of how much he earns because of his name and fame, but how many of you know that Ronaldo's mother was a cook and his father was a gardener? He, too, faced poverty and adversity early on his life. Let's come to the story of our own great super-boxer Mary Kom, five-time World Boxing Champion, Olympic Bronze medalist and first woman Asian Games Gold medalist from India. Her case is no different. Her parents worked in *jhum* fields, surviving on subsistence agriculture, and Mary had to also face a lot of resistance from society for taking up boxing, a sport that has traditionally been considered masculine, the preserve of the male. But magnificent Mary stuck to her goal undeterred while helping her family in the fields *and* studying. In fact, at times, as the mother of a newborn, she would attend to her baby son, who was often feverish, and then run to practice."

There was complete silence in the field.

"But why am I telling you all this now? Just to impress upon you that, before all these champions became gods and goddesses of Indian sport, they were all very normal human beings, like you and me, and many faced more difficulties than you and I can ever imagine. But they all had one unique thing about them that made them unstoppable. Do you know what that was? Indomitable passion, ambition and a never-say-die attitude! It's like they all took a never-quit pledge, stuck to it against all odds in letter and spirit and continued practicing no matter what stood in their way. To others, it seemed that they were obsessed, addicted to their goal—that is what true champions are made of." Vivek took a sip of water. "How many of you have seen the film that showed how Milkha Singh went to the Olympics and made India proud?" Many in the audience raised their hands. "Then you all must be aware of what he had to go through just to get there. Yes, success in the Olympics does not come easy. It requires all-consuming commitment to all-round transformation. You have to develop not just an Olympian goal but an Olympian body, an Olympian mind and an Olympian soul, too. You have to be 100% dedicated and 0% distracted. My role is to provide you with the best physical and mental training, but it is you who will have to do the work and prepare yourself, step by step, for the challenges ahead. Now that you know how people who were once like you and me accomplished such superlative achievements with sheer determination, hard work and non-stop practice, I repeat my question: are you ready for the task ahead?"

"YES!" came the resounding response immediately.

"Can you do it?"

"YES WE CAN!" came the thunderous assertion.

"Who all think they can? Raise your hand!"

Every child listening to Vivek threw a hand up towards the sky.

Divi – Small Town to Sports Hub

Time went by. One morning, when Vivek was sipping tea and enjoying the warm rays of the rising sun and the sight of groups of birds travelling through the clear blue sky, the telephone rang at home. He rose from his easy chair and went to take the call that would prove to be a game-changer.

"Hello," he said, picking up the receiver.

"Good morning, Mr. Vivek. I am the secretary of Mr. S. K. Anand, Sports Minister of the Government of India. The minister will be in Divi tomorrow and would like to meet and interact with you and your team, around 11 a.m."

After his initial elation had passed and he had responded appropriately to this very pleasant surprise, Vivek returned to the balcony and sat back in his chair. Many thoughts came to his mind. *Maybe the time has come. Maybe all our efforts are soon going to pay dividends. Maybe more help will come from the government at the center. Maybe the world is taking note of the meaningful transformations in the lives of the youths I have been working with. Maybe the metamorphosis in the kids, their transformation into potential champions, is not invisible anymore.* In his heart of hearts, he thanked Paresh, himself for his hard work, his friends for their cooperation, the district administration, the businessmen, the women's association and, above all, his "Power 100" special team, all of whom were now part of a revolution that was changing the face of India, day by day, town by town.

The next day, the local media hailed him, his vision, the team and their exceptional performances as "the pride of Divi." Several regional newspapers had put out amusing front page headlines:

"Divi will soon gift India many Olympic champions"

"The man who made a local *samosa* travel the world is now making local talents go global"

"Get ready to see Divi's women make global sports headlines"

"14-year-old small town boy breaks latest Olympic record in 100m sprint"

Vivek's mind wandered towards Divya. They had not met in many days, but she was with him all the time in his thoughts and actions. He could not forget the way she had reacted when he had last spoken to her and informed her of his team's recent achievements. He could hear the happiness in her tone when she congratulated him on the success of his efforts to help the youth, especially girls who had always been ignored for no fault of their own.

Vivek spent hours at night with Paresh, telling him all about his desire to make Divi an Olympic city. Vivek did nothing without talking to Paresh about his plans. Paresh had become something like his God. Vivek knew that he had to move on from *samosas* to the Olympics. Without Paresh, none of it would have been possible.

The next day, Vivek woke up just on time and checked whether the preparations that he had discussed with the event manager, the volunteers, the caterers and the team members the previous day were ready. Satisfied, he took a quick bath and scanned his wardrobe thoroughly for the right dress for the occasion, finally picking his favorite suit along with his favorite blue tie. He had a soft corner for blue, his lucky color. He smiled at the thought that, in spite of his IIT-trained engineer's mind and temperament, he retained such superstitious beliefs. He looked in the mirror one last time and drove to the stadium, smiling all the way.

It was 10:15. The minister would arrive in a mere 45 minutes. The event venue was abuzz with activity. Everything was in place. All the invitees had arrived. Vivek was pleased with the arrangements. The excitement grew with every passing minute.

Someone at the gate shouted, "They're coming! See, a line of cars with red lights!"

Vivek proceeded to the gate, where girls with garlands were already stationed. When the cars pulled up and the dignitaries emerged, they were given a warm, ceremonial welcome and led to their respective places in the meeting hall. After the greetings and exchanges of pleasantries, the business began. The minister and other officials were very appreciative of Vivek's vision and the way it was going. After Vivek gave his presentation, the minister happily agreed to many of his demands, including a substantial monthly stipend for each trainee to boost their morale and ensure the cooperation of their families. The minister even promised more help in the future.

Some of the teammates present in the meeting described their experiences and the changes that had been wrought in them, including their pledge to make the nation proud in the upcoming Olympics. When the time came for refreshments, the mood became more informal. Everybody was cozying up to everybody and engaging in closer interactions while enjoying snacks and coffee. Many spoke highly of Vivek and his vision. Some of the members of the ministerial delegation interacted with the trainee athletes to get to know them better. Vivek was happy to watch all this from a slight distance.

The next day, sitting in his easy chair as usual and enjoying the morning sun, the sky, the birds and his tea, Vivek was feeling more ambitious. Now that he had assurances from the minister, he had lots of work to do. He began planning the day ahead as he finished his tea. He also felt like calling Divya, as he had been unable to the previous day.

Suddenly, a different idea popped up in his mind. *Why don't I spread the movement further? Why settle for this much? After all, visions have no limits, and nor does the willpower of man. Why don't I extend this approach to other areas of personal and national interest?* In his mind, he could see many opportunities to do so in the country, which was materially poor but rich in talent. He had seen as much talent inside the campuses of IIT and IIM as he had outside it. He had seen great potential in cities as well as villages. The traditions and culture of the country were a source of ceaseless wonder to him. *Why not tap the potential? Our weavers, our sculptors, our dancers, our singers, our potters, our varieties of food, our traditional paintings, our traditionally-trained artistic imagination and the gifted hands of our people…how can they be wasted?* These questions made him restless. He thought of inviting his friends to join him and of building a team that would fan out to every corner of India to rediscover its potential and figure out ways of marketing its potential worldwide. Now was the time to start a movement—if he could do it with *samosas* and the Olympics team, he could do it with any project. He sighed with relief and thought the time had come to start the movement in a big way. *I will discuss it with Divya, maybe tonight*, he thought, knowing fully well what a great support she would again be.

A Social Thinker

Vivek was a visionary but his vision was buried under a thick, unfathomable crust of formalities. During his childhood, he was forced by his parents, and by circumstances, to become a conformist. The habit persisted in his adulthood, too. As a consequence, he lost his original creative restlessness. But living in that small township had washed away that confining crust. His mind was now more open, vibrant and observant. Though his personal life might have been dull and the environment commonplace, Vivek was sure of the possibilities and potential it possessed.

Professionally, there was no stopping him. The people he had met and the conversations he had had in the last couple of years had made him come alive with unusual possibilities. His heart went out to the people he saw who could live much better lives but had been languishing only because systems and belief-patterns were moving in an endless cycle no one was willing to break. He thought of the woman he had once seen with just one *sari*, the people who waited in hospital queues for basic medicines, in schools without educational material, and of the beautiful town that had no convenient place to sit and relax. The list turned his mind into a fountainhead of ideas, but all of them had taken a backseat to Matru ka Samosa.

He knew he had to begin somewhere to address these issues. He had already begun exploring ways of adding to the beautification of the town. To kickstart his neglected ideas and convert them into a successful project, he contacted the District Collector first.

"Sir, I request you to grant me the permission to execute some of my ideas for the beautification of this small township and a number of villages around it on government land and plots," said Vivek.

The Collector looked blankly at him. "I don't think that's possible."

"It depends on you."

"How so?"

"Your word is final."

"I can't risk government land on private plans."

"The land isn't at risk in any way. I'll just be a representative of the government."

"What do you mean by that?"

"I'll work for the beautification of the neglected parks and barren pieces of land here," said Vivek confidently.

The Collector was impressed. Vivek's academic qualifications, enthusiasm and confidence hinted at immense possibilities. "The idea appeals to me," he said.

"We won't be using government resources at any level," Vivek added. "However, the government will be kept informed of the progress and implementation of all our plans. You will be our titular sponsor. We will respect your authority but…"

"But what?" the Collector asked.

"I request you to keep us safe from any official and political interference."

"I can promise you that."

Vivek thanked the Collector. Passing him some sheets of paper, he said, "Here is a blueprint of our plans and a list of possible sponsors."

Going through the papers, the Collector said, "Your proposal offers the promise of betterment. As far as I'm concerned, I promise you a carte blanche."

***

Vivek once again contacted his old friends and acquaintances; those who were technically qualified and experts in their respective fields. Some well-known businesspeople also promised help to him. A mega plan was drawn up and the process of implementation began in earnest.

It was a time-bound project. Old spots in town were given a facelift and new structures were sanctioned. People who needed employment were provided dignified jobs with reliable pay structures. The best thing about it was that there were neither any underhand practices nor any personal agendas or ulterior motives. It was, in fact, the people's crusade against existing narrow-minded concepts.

Vivek's efforts brought about revolutionary changes in Divi, transforming it and the villages around it into a tourist spot and also a spot for recreation, away from the hullabaloo of the city. In a matter of one year, Vivek's vision brought about a complete change in the lifestyle of the local people. Such were the changes there that the place became a model for the whole country and soon began to attract the attention of urban sociologists and town planners.

The Collector had become a friend of Vivek's. Being a bureaucrat, he was able to grasp Vivek's vision thoroughly. He understood why life in that township had charmed Vivek. Before coming to Divi, he, like Vivek, had not entertained any positive opinions about the intellectual abilities of rural people, but both of them had changed their opinions now.

Now, Vivek was of the opinion that, by using all available resources, he could bring about much-needed changes. He was now thinking of developing the place into an educational hub. He began a small institute for students aspiring to get into IITs and IIMs and started conducting classes himself while looking for teachers to hire. Some of his friends from IIT were willing to help him by coming to Divi for short periods to teach and guide the students.

Vivek was very free with his students. He never stopped them from asking any questions.

Once, a student said, "Sir, I want to ask you something."

"Sure."

"Sir, why have you come to this place?"

Vivek laughed and said, "To create big opportunities for you."

Another student got up. "Sir!"

"Yes?"

"Do you think we'll make it big someday?"

"Remember one thing: there isn't any substitute for hard work."

"Thank you, sir. I think I have got my answer."

He said to the students, "A number of my friends from IIT and IIM have promised me that they will come here from time to time to guide you. I'm sure their coaching will expand your mind."

One student said, "Sir, we won't let you down in any way."

A girl got up. "Sir, I'm very happy that you have given me a chance to study here. I'll put in every effort to crack the entrance test for IIT."

Vivek said, "I want all of you to put in your best efforts and, one day, when you yourself become an able technocrat, then you must spare at least some time for the betterment of any place where the students are deprived of opportunities." His eyes glowed with a strange passion. He went on, "If all of us begin thinking about others, a time will come when the very face of this country will change. It's my conviction that all educated young people must go and work for some time in rural areas. By doing that, they'll make their country prosperous and, by making their country prosperous, they will become more prosperous, too."

Vivek also thought of creating opportunities for people to earn money. Towards this end, his IIM-trained mind began planning intensely. The Collector had approved his overall plan for beautification in totality. Vivek did not demand any money from the government. This plan was to develop the floriculture in the area. The place was full of beautiful flowers and exotic plants. Besides that, Vivek also paid a lot of attention to rainwater harvesting. In the beginning, people were a bit skeptical of his plans, but when the results began showing, they were impressed. Now, they devoted themselves wholeheartedly to implementing the plan. The floriculture soon brought about prosperity for the people.

A number of beautiful parks also came up. The use of topiary art did a lot for the place. Some of the parks were so beautiful that tourists began coming to the place in droves. This resulted in good business opportunities for the people.

This venture also gave him a chance to explore his long-forgotten dream of being a musician. Although he hadn't learned music, he still appreciated it. So he devised a plan to have various *ragas* played in the parks and gardens at various times of the day, through soft, mellow speakers that did not jar and trouble the visitors. The entire vibe of the forgotten little town of Divi had got a makeover.

The best thing about it was that the people of the area had now realized their own potential. The whole region and its inhabitants, through their skills and creativity, had begun getting appreciation from all and sundry. The city thanked Vivek for his efforts at bringing about a qualitative change in the lifestyle of the people and introduced them to possibilities that they had not been not aware of until then. What had started as a small venture on Vivek's part had grown into a giant model for all sociologists and planners to take note of.

A Reflection on Life

Matru ka Samosa was still the biggest source of contentment for Vivek. It was a unique phenomenon in the eyes of market analysts. For some of them, the phenomenal popularity of the brand suggested new and unforeseen possibilities in Indian business. It stood for the dynamic nature of a well-planned business strategy, on the one hand, and, on the other, it suggested that nothing was too small to be overlooked by anyone in any situation.

All said and done, it was more than a brand for the people in general. For them, it also meant that an alliance between two diverse elements could generate huge opportunities. Vivek and Paresh had perplexed the entire business community. They had become two bright stars in the entrepreneurial firmament. Young entrepreneurs looked up to them. The relentless expansion of their chain had become a great saga of innovative and imaginative business.

If Vivek was a visionary planner, Paresh was a steadfast and determined worker. It was a rare partnership between two individuals who were poles apart in every way. Those around them wondered how a highly educated and competent person could get along with a person who had neither much education nor any sophistication.

Vivek was now a celebrity. His old friends often dropped in on him and talked about various things. Vivek was now an icon to them. He tried to convince his friends that Paresh himself was a dynamic person and emphasized the role Paresh had played in Vivek's life.

"Paresh has been my main prop in life. He's the one who has made me realize how precious one's life is," Vivek once told one of his friends.

"You seem to have a lot of appreciation for him," said the friend. "It makes no sense to me. What appeals to you most in him?"

"He's a very dynamic person," said Vivek instantly.

"How did you two meet?" the friend asked Vivek.

"Destiny!"

"Tell me more!"

Vivek said, "I'd lost my will to fight. I don't know why, but I'd become indifferent to life. My personal life had become intolerable. I met Paresh in a train. He sensed my internal chaos and, in the darkest moment of my life, he became my prop. He gave me shelter and nursed me back to sanity and stability."

"It sounds like some romance."

"To make a long story short, both of us seemed to be destined to help each other. So, when my mind had begun to think clearly, I suggested to Paresh that he expand his business. Initially, he didn't have much faith in anything I suggested, but he trusted me. In his own way, he has a tremendous mind." After a pause, Vivek, continued, "Today, in my opinion, the youth should cultivate a dynamic approach towards life. I feel the word success must be redefined."

"You redefine it, with Paresh," the friend taunted.

"I will," said Vivek confidently. "In today's context, we need a total change in our way of thinking and social values. The youth must look for unexplored and unconventional avenues. If a job isn't available, don't cry over it! There are myriad other things for you to do. They can transform themselves from job seekers to job givers. I say that with the authority of my experience. Once, while passing through a busy market, I saw a young girl cleaning the window of a skyscraper, on the 16th floor. This, in my view, is the real spirit of adventure. I'm sure if this spirit is cultivated in the youth of this country then the problem of unemployment won't bother anyone."

Impressed, the friend asked, "And what measures do you suggest to the planners?"

"I can think of only one right now that will bring about the desired change in the psyche of the youth," said Vivek with confidence and certainty.

"And what is it?"

Vivek said, "Bring about a total change in our educational setup and reorient the thinking process at childhood. It's my conviction that this country is sure to move towards a social and cultural revolution in the coming times. I foresee a bright future. There are moments when I feel, or rather, I'm sure that a bold and unconventional leadership will effect the desired results. Our march towards global standards as a society is no more just a vague and idealistic dream. It's right before us now, in a tangible form. The youth isn't looking for narrow and parochial structures. They want to be global participants."

When Vivek stopped, the friend said, "Your statement has given me a new insight into the crux of the problem. Thanks!"

"I trust the youth and their capabilities," said Vivek.

"The darkness around them isn't going to last forever," said the friend.

"The youth is ambitious and talented. They just need true leadership. Given wings, they'll touch the sky," said Vivek effusively. "The youth can think for themselves. Each youth is full of untapped and unexplored energy looking for an outlet. The global political system today is the greatest pollutant in the human system. It has threatened the very existence of mankind with its ulterior motives. Youthful ambitions and activities are harmless, but they take on a vicious and gigantic form when they're directed by those who have become devoid of all human emotions."

Vivek fell silent. His friend said anything. Maybe he was experiencing a transformation. He wondered if Vivek was right. He felt that he had been living in a dark world. He also felt that the youth could no longer be overlooked. All over the world, young people were misguided by the system and being led into chaos and destruction.

"Vivek, I thank you from the depths of my heart," said the friend, looking at Vivek with a sense of growing respect.

"What for?" asked Vivek.

"For clearing out the old set of values from my mind. You've given me an expansive perspective of the whole issue," said the friend. "You're absolutely right in pointing out that there has been a steep decline in our systems of civilization. Your invocation of youth power is a very creative suggestion."

His voice full of warmth, Vivek thanked his friend profusely and said, "I am glad you understand my point of view. I've just pointed out how all our contemporary evils and illnesses have their origin in the distribution of resources. Because of wrong guidance, the impulsive youth has been marching down the path of destruction. While the aim is to wipe out all injustice and evil in the world, what is required is profound contemplation of the goals. The potential of the youth is infinite—if properly identified and redirected, they can change the destiny of mankind and the world. I believe that the youth alone will go through a process of intellectual and spiritual distillation and set right everything on the globe."

A Lover's Confession

Vivek was set on a process of intense thinking. He had begun brooding over the larger issues of the world and of mankind. He had withdrawn from the business activities of day-to-day life. His growing apathy did not escape the attention of Paresh. It disturbed him very much. However, he did not express his feelings to Vivek overtly.

One day, when the two of them were sitting together, Vivek, closely observing Paresh's face, said, "Paresh what's wrong with you? You're looking so off color!"

Paresh mumbled, "I'm all right, my friend. Nothing is wrong with me."

"Something is definitely wrong with you. I've known you for quite some time. You can't conceal your feelings. Now tell me what's bothering you," insisted Vivek.

Paresh was about to let out his secret fears when his wife came in and handed over a sealed letter to Vivek. It had the stamp of Government of India. Filled with curiosity, Vivek opened it and quickly went through it.

"By God! It's just unimaginable."

"What is it?" both Paresh and his wife asked together, full of curiosity.

"The Government of India wants to award me the Padma Shri. I don't think I deserve it at all!" Then, looking at Paresh intensely, he observed, "They should give this award to you. You're the more deserving person for it in my view."

"I'm nothing before you, *babuji*. Whatever I am today, it's just because of you. Before meeting you, I was just an ordinary and unknown *samosawala* in a small township," said Paresh with the utmost humility.

His humility did not appeal to Vivek. Rejecting it completely, he said, "Paresh, do I have to remind you that you're now a global figure? You're a youth icon today. I'm nothing before you."

What Vivek was failing to see was that he was the one who had been more engaged in social activities. He helped talented and brilliant students who did not have the resources to be coached crack competitive exams like the IIT-JEE for free. He had also adopted a village in which to carry out his work and, through his skillful management, he had transformed it. He had transformed Divi from a small town to an Olympic town, a sports hub. The result was that it became a model for all the towns of the country. The best concepts of a perfect township had been applied to the makeover of the village.

All of this made him a natural choice for the prestigious national award.

"Paresh, I'll see that you, too, get an award of this kind for having created such a big setup here in this country. You've given employment to so many people in your enterprise. I feel it's a great source of inspiration to people at large. Some of our most brilliant and successful people have had humble beginnings," said Vivek is a warm and highly emotional tone.

Paresh said, "I don't want to challenge you. I don't have any delusions about myself. I know who I am and what I was before meeting you. Whatever you say about me, I accept with humility. I feel proud. But, you must also accept the veracity of my statement!"

A benevolent smile flashed across Vivek's face. Looking at Paresh, he asked, "What's your statement?"

Paresh did not answer immediately. Perhaps he was thinking of the most effective way to put it. At last, breaking a long silence, he blurted out, "I'm fully aware of my limitations. I don't have any false sense of importance either. The truth is you're the plinth I stand on. So, never ever think of going away from me, from here. Your presence is vital for me. Without you, I feel incomplete."

"Nonsense!" said Vivek, amused and laughing.

"Why do you say that? Do you doubt my sincerity?"

"No, not at all."

"Then how could you utter that word?"

Putting one hand on Paresh's shoulder, Vivek said, his voice very sweet, "Now, don't throw tantrums. My dear Paresh, you must know quite well that, when your business has grown to this dimension, you mustn't worry too much about looking after it, running it. Your top executives are there to look after it. As for me, I'll always be there with you."

"I have been a dullard throughout my life," said Paresh. "I hadn't even dreamt of such vastness. Earlier, everything was limited to selling a few *samosas*, but now, it involves all sorts of complexities. All these activities now mean knowing the changing trends of the market and the appropriate marketing. How do I handle all these challenges effectively?"

An amused Vivek said, "Oh Paresh, you're incorrigible! Just keep an eye on expenditure and income. You're extremely good at that, better than others, without any doubt. Everything else will go on smoothly. Trust me! I'm always with you. Any further discussion over it will annoy me. Now be calm and prepared to face all the challenges ahead!"

Paresh smiled like a child. He was calm. He could perceive clearly that there was an essential affinity between them in spite of a surface-level polarity.

***

It was midnight. Vivek was awoken by the ringing of his mobile.

"Hello!" he said, answering.

"How are you, my dear?" It was Divya's voice. A sweetness coursed through him.

"Hello, Divya, how's everything at your end?" he asked in an even voice, trying to control the warmth that he felt on hearing her words.

"Why don't you take a guess?"

"You know I'm not very good at guessing things."

"I'm angry with you. You've left me out!"

"How so?"

"You're a real funny one!"

"Explain."

"You've got the Padma Shri and I'm hearing about it through the media! That pained me. How am I your soulmate then?"

"I have doubts about whether I deserve it. It didn't make sense talking about it without being sure," said Vivek.

"You're getting this award for your social service in rural India, my dear *samosawala*, you aren't getting it for your *samosas*! You're getting rewarded for your commitment to bettering the lives of left-behind villagers," Divya reasoned.

"I should have told you. I'll accept it as my worst failure. I apologize to you unconditionally," Vivek said.

"Apology accepted, even though it sounds so uptight," she said in her pleasantest tone.

"Divya, I forget things…even you, sometimes."

Her sweet laughter rang out again. "Now don't feign indifference. I know you well, you poseur!"

"Divya!"

"Yes!"

"I don't know how to convey my feelings to you."

"Don't hesitate! Just speak," said Divya seductively.

"All night long, I keep thinking about you. Although you're away from me in a foreign land, I feel your presence beside me all the time," whispered Vivek like a passionate lover.

"Vivek, I want to tell you something, too."

"Yes, tell me."

"I don't know how to put my exact feelings across to you in an original way," she said, somewhat confused.

"At least make an effort," said Vivek.

"I'm at a loss."

"Just speak."

"Before I say anything, I want to ask you a question."

"Okay. I'll try to answer it as convincingly as possible."

Reassured, Divya said, "I feel all genuine lovers are poor speakers. Why do you think that is?"

"It's very simple," he said.

"Seems difficult to me."

"I'm not very sure about it either, but I can make a guess, although it's a bit risky," said Vivek.

"I feel it's because lovers are governed by their feelings and emotions," she said.

"Maybe. They look for happiness in each other."

"Do lovers give happiness to each other?"

"In my view, they do," said Vivek with certainty.

"Lovers are unpredictable," she said rather illogically.

"What do you mean by that, Divya? It seems like a meaningless statement."

"I want to confess something to you."

"Divya, I want to tell you something, too."

"Yes?"

"You own me," said Vivek. "There are moments when I feel I'm a prisoner to your charm!"

"Since you have expressed your feelings so candidly, I must also tell you what I feel about you," she said in a delighted voice.

"We have been talking like two persons who have fallen in love for the first time," Vivek said. "I feel like an inexperienced lover."

"Vivek, genuine lovers are always inexperienced!"

"How so?" he asked.

"Simple! For a genuine lover, each moment with the loved one is a new, fresh experience," she explained.

He then said, "That's because love is infinite. It's intoxicating. Lovers can give up anything, even the most precious things, when they're seeking each other."

Divya was overcome with powerful emotions. She said, "Vivek, in the silence of the night, I keep dreaming about you. I keep dreaming that if I'd had wings, I'd fly into your stable and comforting arms!"

Vivek whispered, "Divya, before you, I'm neither a mentor nor a planner. Outwardly, I'm stable and calm, I don't show any sign of the chaos within me. As far as my nights are concerned, they're meaningless. My real self is somehow connected to you, and I'm thankful for that."

Divya said philosophically, "Our togetherness is our perfection in the vast desert of life. I wish you all the happiness in the world."

"Be happy, my love! You're the one who's made me soft again after the world had hardened me."

"This talk has relieved me. See you soon!" she whispered hypnotically.

Moments of Harmony

Paresh had very small dreams in life and the money and fame that he was getting did not affect him at all. He did not understand all the commotion around him. What was he doing that made people see him in a different light and as an important person? He thought of himself as just an ordinary *samosa* maker trying to make a living for himself and those working for him. He was just not able to fathom what all the hullabaloo surrounding him was about. Every time a news channel approached him, he would shyly refuse to give them any sound bites. He was too shy to get himself videographed.

He often complained to Vivek that he did not wish to be that important. He would tell Vivek that it was Vivek who was the real star, as all this was the result of his hard work, but Vivek in return would try to make him understand that the real vision and labor were and would always be Paresh's, so it made complete sense that people wanted to know more about him.

Neither wanted to bask in the glory of fame and limelight, yet they stood rock-solid for each other. Both of them thought the other person worthier and would happily pass the baton to the other whenever the need to step in front as the real hero of the show arose. Vivek was not greedy for money as he had been born into it; he detested it. For Paresh, all this was never on his mind. All he was bothered about was whether his customers liked what they ate and appreciated his skills. To him, the love and support of Vivek, his family and the thousands of *samosa* eaters all over the country was all the reward he ever wanted and he was content with it.

Meanwhile, Vivek had begun receiving calls from friends regarding the Padma Shri. Although it took him time to understand what he'd done to achieve the honor, when he did, he felt a profound sense of humility. It wasn't what he had been looking for, but when he received it, he realized how tremendous the opportunity fate had granted him was.

During his long talks and discussions with his friends, Paresh and Divya, he gradually realized that the passion with which he had worked in Divi, not just for Matru ka Samosa, but also for the community in general, had been noticed. He understood that his sincere efforts to develop cooperative horticulture, healthcare, school education and cleanliness projects in the village had made a huge impact. People had been coming to and studying the systems in Divi, but he had only met them to help them understand what they needed to. It had never occurred to him that his work would set a memorable example for the youth. It really was a humbling thought.

To add to his fulfillment, Vivek's love life had bloomed into an exquisite experience of the soul. He would, three times a week, go and meet Divya and they would chat for hours. She had even invited him to her home and introduced him to her parents. He liked the small and loving family that she came from. They were warm, friendly and open to accepting people as their own. He felt at home with Divya and her parents, and would often go on weekends to meet them for lunch or tea. With Divya's support and love, he was able to forgive and forget Reeta. He told her that, soon, he would initiate talks of marriage with her parents and officially ask for their consent to marry her.

His relation with his mother also got better with the passage of time. He was at peace with her and often called her and talked to her. He even told her about Divya and about his plans to marry her. She was happy with the developments in his life and thought it was time he moved on in life and entered a phase of familial bliss.

The more Vivek was getting to do what he always wanted to, the more positive his attitude towards life became. Now, small everyday matters did not aggravate him. All the bitterness was dispelled from his system; he was a refined man now. He started ignoring the negatives and embracing the better things in life. The laughter he shared with Divya mattered more to him than the stress he would feel after work. Every day, when he returned home from work, he would call Divya. It served as a stress-buster for him. He certainly was a different man now. He would smile more often, crack jokes and try pulling Paresh's leg in a friendly manner all the time. He would take care of his fitness routine and go out jogging in the mornings, as a result of which he was much leaner, fitter and had regained his youthful good looks. He felt more energetic and charged up about life and work. The correct decision that he had made, to get off the train that one morning, had helped him get his life back on track and he would always be thankful for that.

Much to Paresh's discomfort, he was being contacted by all and sundry since his business had become a sensation the world over. He was quite comfortable in his small world; this recognition made him immensely uneasy. Vivek tried his best to make him see the situation from the eyes of the observer.

A man from nowhere had claimed his due and was now everywhere. Every newspaper, every media channel was talking about just one man: Paresh Kashyap. Everyone wanted to know more about him. In him, many youngsters found great inspiration. For them, he was a paradigm of determination and focus. Every owner of small sweets-and-snacks shops wanted to be like him. Every small shopowner wanted to copy his business model and become as rich and successful as he was. To those people, he was a hero, a beacon of hope. He gave them inspiration: *if he can, then so can we.* Matru ka Samosa was soon gripping the nation in all its glory and Paresh and Vivek were only too happy to have succeeded in such a manner. More than the money and fame, it was the fact that what they had set out to do in the beginning was accomplished and they were now being hailed for their quality of work.

One day, while both Vivek and Paresh were busy at the factory, which had become an extension of their workshop, Vivek received a call. It was from the Secretary of the Indian Institute of Business Studies, Pune. He wanted to invite Paresh to be a guest speaker at his institute. At first thrilled at the offer, Vivek hesitated to say yes to the Secretary immediately, fearing Paresh would never agree to it. He knew Paresh ran away from any kind of public adulation or exposure and to make him consent to a thing like this was almost impossible. Vivek knew he would be required to do some heavy duty persuading before he could make Paresh say yes; still, he was not too sure. However, not willing to let go of the opportunity so easily either, he asked the secretary to give him some time and said he would get back to him after speaking with Paresh, to which the secretary readily agreed.

Vivek knew that getting Paresh to agree would be tricky, but realized it would be equally difficult to prepare him for the talk, and disastrous, without fully readying him to meet a group that exclusive. The next two days were spent by Vivek hatching a plan to introduce Paresh to his new audience of young and budding future entrepreneurs. Doing all the homework in secrecy, Vivek kept Paresh out of the picture.

Oblivious of Vivek's secret work, Paresh kept going about his daily chores. While observing his body language and mannerisms, Vivek reached the conclusion that there was a lot that Paresh would have to be trained in, in terms of social etiquette, before he could go out there as the confident businessman that the rest of the world took him for. At night, Vivek broke the news to Paresh that, after two weeks, both of them had to go to Pune, where Paresh, for the first time, would be heading a panel as a guest speaker at one of India's leading business schools.

Although Paresh had, to an extent, learned the ways of the world and was slowly and gradually improving his social quotient, he was still not quite there. He lacked the refinement required by a man of the stature he had. The world wanted to see him in a certain mold and he was still far from achieving that. He required a lot more work as he had yet not been sufficiently exposed to the world. Though his products were making news everywhere, he was not well-travelled or well-read. Vivek knew it would require a bit of patience and hard work bringing Paresh to that level and he was prepared to put in that amount of time and effort. Although he had just two weeks, he was determined to make Paresh at least reasonably presentable, if nothing more.

"Congrats, Paresh!"

"For what, *babuji*?"

"You have become a famous person now!"

This alerted Paresh to the fact that Vivek was hinting at something. "Do you want to tell me something?" he asked Vivek.

"Yes."

"Tell me, *babuji*," Paresh said, full of uncertainty.

"I'm not very happy with you," said Vivek in a neutral tone.

This disturbed Paresh. "Please forgive me if I've offended you in any way."

Gently, Vivek put one hand on Paresh's shoulder and said, "Aren't we friends?"

"Yes we are, *babuji*, why do you doubt it?"

"Then why do you keep calling me *babuji*? I feel terrible about it. Why should there be any formality between friends?"

Paresh did not speak for a few moments. He did not know how to pacify Vivek. Then, breaking a long silence, he said, "I was a small and insignificant person once. You raised my status and bestowed this elegance upon me. All my present renown and grace are because of you."

Vivek said, "And never, ever forget how *you* saved *my* life. *You* were the one who helped *me* step out of darkness. Whatever I've done for you is nothing before what you have done for me. Now, listen, I have some good news for you."

Paresh was confused. "Tell me if you think it will be of some use to me."

A wide smile spread over Vivek's face. Beaming with happiness, he said, "You have been invited to address the students at the Indian Institute of Business Studies, Pune."

The moment those words came out of Vivek's mouth, Paresh lost his composure. Almost stammering, he said, "*Babuji*, don't ask me to do that!"

"Why not?" asked Vivek with anger.

Paresh said, teary-eyed and with utmost difficulty, "I'm sure that I'll be a great failure in the midst of that learned gathering." He paused, looking for some reasonable explanation that would satisfy Vivek. All of a sudden, an idea flashed across Paresh's mind. Putting on a conciliatory smile, he said, with pauses and in almost an inaudible voice, "I've just been a *samosa* maker all through my life. Ask me to make any kind of *samosa* and I can do it most perfectly. But delivering a speech before a gathering will undermine and destroy my very self." He paused again. All the while, he seemed to have been groping for convincing words. "Okay, I have a very workable suggestion!"

Vivek knew that Paresh was completely flummoxed. Even so, he asked, "And what is your bright suggestion, my dear friend?"

Paresh said, rather cheerfully, "Divide the whole thing into two parts."

"How?"

"You address them and say all those bright things that will make them successful at everything they do."

"And what will you do?" asked Vivek.

An innocent smile came over Paresh's face. In his sweetest tone, he said, "I'll tell them, show them, how to make delicious *samosas*."

Vivek guffawed. Paresh looked at him nonplussed. Vivek was amused at his friend's innocence. Then, in a serious tone, Vivek said, "My dear Paresh, you're such a simple person. You don't even know how big a figure you've become in the business world. People all over the country, mainly from the business world and students of business management, want to learn the secrets that have made you so big in such a short time and, that too, from such humble beginnings. In their eyes, you're a phenomenon. They want to explore their own capabilities through your advice and tips. Those youngsters out there are full of dreams and want to take after you in their life's battle. You can't turn your back on them. Moreover, I must make it very clear to you that there cannot be any going back on it at this stage. So, my dear friend, gird up your loins and begin preparing for the occasion."

Looking desperate, Paresh said rather miserably, "Okay, as you wish. If you think I can do it then I'll try to put in my best efforts."

With extreme tenderness Vivek said, "Paresh, be confident, I trust your abilities. I am sure you'll be successful. My dear friend, remember that I'll be with you through it all, backing you up."

Vivek's words helped Paresh relax. Vivek was a great fan of Paresh's abilities. From the very beginning, he had seen the steely resolve in his friend. Although outwardly he seemed to be a very simple man, he was in essence not a man without imagination and vision; once assured of a thing, he would take it to its conclusion.

The process of Paresh's makeover began in earnest. The emphasis was mainly on restoring his confidence in himself. Vivek connected the process of grooming to the success of Matru ka Samosa.

"From now on, you're going to call me Vivek," Vivek firmly told Paresh, like a dictator. Paresh looked distressed. Seeing that expression on his friend's face amused Vivek inwardly, but he kept his own face impassive so as not to dissipate the effect of his words. "I'm done with your calling me *babuji* all the time. You'd better change your style or else our friendship comes to an end." He stopped again to read Paresh's reaction. Paresh was now totally at sea. Looking lovingly at his friend, Vivek said, "Now be a good boy and call me Vivek."

Paresh did not speak immediately. He kept brooding over the difficult situation. Vivek's gaze was fixed on his face. Paresh knew that Vivek could be adamant on certain occasions and about specific issues. With his voice choking up, he could only whisper, "I'll try it, though it's a very difficult task for me!"

"Try it, then," said Vivek.

"Vi...vek," Paresh uttered almost plaintively.

Vivek's face broke into a smile. He said, "Now, my dear friend Paresh, you've to practice it a 100 times a day. I'm sure it'll become a part of your life. You'll soon be very comfortable with it. It's going to be so spontaneous within days that you'll laugh at your own earlier gaucherie."

"Thanks, boss…Vivek" said Paresh. "You're such a strict disciplinarian. I hate it!"

Vivek laughed. "This is very encouraging, my dear friend," he said. He waited for a few moments. "We're now up to our necks in it. There isn't any escape for us. You'll soon become the most sought-after person around! I'm very excited about it. I wish you the best, and let me assure you, you deserve all the kudos that are coming to you."

"What if I fail, Vivek? It will be the first big failure in my life!" said Paresh, his voice full of genuine concern.

Face calm and tone even, Vivek said, "My dearest Paresh, today I'm going to tell you the greatest truth in life. Money and success are the most powerful commodities in this materialistic world. One's resourcefulness is the guarantee of one's position in society. The more resourceful a person is, the more the public appreciates him or her."

Paresh had now an intense look in his eyes. Slowly, his face broke into a guileless smile. He spoke with a surge of emotions, "Yes, commander, I'll follow your lead."

His simplicity touched Vivek's heart. Looking at Paresh affectionately, he said, "Paresh, I know very well that nothing is beyond your ambit. In my estimation, you're the wisest master of everyday life I've met."

Paresh was delighted when he saw the affectionate expression in the eyes of his friend. The two friends remained quiet for some time. A soft silence seemed to have spread over the place.

"*Babuji*, my father was my only mentor and guide initially. He constantly kept drumming into my ears: 'Never ever be ashamed of your status in life. Be proud of your skills. Your devotion to your skill and art will help you rise above your complexes.' He was a strong person. Those coming in contact with him were always affected by his dynamic philosophy."

Vivek replied, "Paresh, I greatly appreciate what your father has taught you, which is reflected in the kind of person you are and have become. But I request you to understand and accept, once and for all, what I'm going to say to you." Paresh looked at his friend with curiosity. "There are moments when I feel, in all sincerity, that you're the person who I've learned the most about life from. I accept you as my guru in those moments."

Overcome with intense emotion, Paresh took Vivek's hands in his. "*Babuji*, thanks! You've elevated the status of a small *samosa* maker today." There was a tremor in Paresh's voice.

Embracing him, Vivek said, "Your *samosas* have driven the world crazy. The time is now ripe, my dearest friend, to make it clear to all young future entrepreneurs of the world that nothing is paltry and meaningless in the vast arena of life, that endless opportunities and possibilities have been lying before them all the time. To know one's real worth is only possible through confident and observant eyes."

Expansion

It would not be wrong to say that human life is full of surprises. There are often events beyond the control of an individual. There are moments when one broods over them and wonders about the unexpectedness with which they occur in one's life. Vivek recalled how one such event had taken place in the life of Paresh. It was a phone call from the office of the Railway Minister.

"Mr. Paresh Kashyap?"

"Yes, speaking."

"The Minster wants to talk to you," a female voice said.

"Talk to me?" Paresh's voice choked up.

"Yes."

"You must have made some mistake. Why should the minister want to talk to me?" asked Paresh nervously.

"There isn't any mistake on our part. Just talk to the minster and everything will be clear to you," said the lady on the other end.

"Okay, I'm on the line," said Paresh with utmost reluctance.

Someone said with a laugh, "Mr. Paresh Kashyap, Ravi Prasad here. How do you do?"

"*Namaskar*, sir."

"*Namaskar!*"

"How can I be of service to you, sir?"

"Mr. Paresh, I'm a big fan of your *samosas*!"

"Thank you, sir! So kind of you!"

"Would you be free at seven p.m. on the coming Monday?"

"Anything I can do for you, sir?"

"Yes, something very special!"

"Tell me, sir."

"You'll have to come over to my place on the appointed day for that."

"I'll be there, sir."

"Great!"

"Sir?"

"Yes?"

"I'm honored."

"Your visit will be my pleasure, but I must tell you something right now," the minister said in a deep voice.

"Yes, sir?"

The minister laughed and said, "Don't come without four of your *samosas*, and do come with Vivek, your mentor, about whom I have been reading so much in the newspapers."

When Paresh told Vivek about his conversation with the minister, Vivek was delighted. The two friends reached the minister's residence right on time on the appointed day. They felt very proud when Ravi Prasad received them personally at the entrance. Ravi Prasad was a man of vision. He made the whole visit very informal. It gave the impression of being a private gathering. His family members were also present there; his wife, son and daughter.

"Here are the owners of Matru Ka Samosa, my new friends, Mr. Paresh Kashyap and Mr. Vivek Kapoor," Ravi Prasad said to them.

Greetings were exchanged. Ravi Prasad was a very sophisticated person. Vivek knew that he was a former professor of Economics at the University of Allahabad. Shalini, his wife, was a well-known writer.

"We're very fond of having MKS with our evening tea," said Shalini with a very warm smile. Turning towards her children, she added, "Ayan and Vimmie can't have their tea without your *samosas*."

"We request you all to keep giving us the same warmth and love," said Vivek, looking at each family member in turn.

"We'll always try to meet your expectations, madam," added Paresh enthusiastically.

Meanwhile, the Aviation Minster, Ajay Kumar, arrived with his wife, Anubha. They were family friends and neighbors, too. Ravi Prasad introduced Paresh and Vivek to the couple.

The wives of the ministers seemed to be very fond of cooking. "I love eating your *samosas*," said Shalini to Vivek and Paresh. "I request you to give me tips about making *samosas* at home."

"I'm also eager to learn about the art of making *samosas*," said Anubha.

Ravi Prasad said, "That can wait. Right now, let us have some tea with the *samosas* that our guests have brought for us."

Everyone clapped at the proposal. Paresh and Vivek were overwhelmed by the ministers' amicability. Tea was brought in and the *samosas* were served.

Suddenly, Vimmie asked Vivek, "Uncle, why do you pack your *samosas* in fours?"

"I, too, am curious about this," said Anubha.

"Nothing very special. Four *samosas* is the standard serving for a family of four at tea time," said Paresh, looking at the kid.

"Thanks!" said Ayan.

When tea was over, the family members of the ministers excused themselves and went inside. Paresh and Vivek were now left with the two ministers. It was time to discuss more important issues.

Ravi Prasad said, "Let's get down to brass tacks, shall we? I want to make a proposal to you both. An offer. It's for you to accept or reject it. However, I'm convinced that you will accept it." Paresh and Vivek were now very alert. An expansive smile appeared on the countenance of the minister. "My proposal is that you supply your pack of four *samosas* to all important railway stations and on all the important trains of our country. I'm sure the venture will be a big hit!"

Ajay Kumar said, "Among all eatables, the *samosa* is the most popular. It forms a significant part of our culinary culture. MKS will be a craze in the coming times!"

Looking at Ravi Prasad, Vivek said, "Thank you, sir!"

"We'll give you our best product, sir," said Paresh with gratitude.

Ajay Kumar cut in. "You can't get away with this deal so lightly."

Vivek and Paresh looked at the Aviation Minister questioningly.

He smiled and, with a mischievous look in his eyes, said, "You must also supply *samosas* at our airports and on our flights. Are you both willing to accept my offer, too?"

"Yes, sir!" Vivek and Paresh said in unison.

Ajay Kumar went on, "It'll boost your business in a big way and thereby the economy of the country. It'll create job opportunities, too, in my view. Ventures like yours, which are related to day-to-day life, may not be mega in size, but they do give employment to thousands."

When Ajay had stopped, Ravi Prasad observed, "Anything accepted by society and the people at large contains huge possibilities for expansion. Matru ka Samosa is on the verge of taking on the status of an international brand is my gut feeling."

Ajay Kumar added, his tone full of warmth, "I've made this offer to you today, but my mind was made up long back, when I first ate your *samosas* at a friend's place."

Ravi Prasad said, "Although the *samosa* has been a part of our everyday life, you're the ones who have bestowed upon it a new refinement and dignity."

Ajay Kumar said, "I can say most authoritatively that anything directed towards making the customer happy is sure to be appreciated by the people. The trend of the market is the voice of the people. This philosophy should be a part of any commercial venture, however small it may be in size to begin with." He stopped and looked at Vivek and Paresh. "I wish you both all the success in the world."

Ravi Prasad had a tremendous sense of humor. He said, "See how Matru ka Samosa is now ruling over the people." Together, they all laughed. A positive radiance seemed to have enveloped them. The outcome of the meeting represented the changing face of the country.

The Disciple is Ready for the Test

From the next morning onwards, Vivek spent three hours every day with Paresh, trying to teach him basic etiquette. He taught him how to greet people and what to say when they inquired about him. He taught him table manners, a few expressions in English so that he could converse with ease and also did a trial run of the speech he had prepared for him. Even though Paresh found it all very exhausting, he, like an obedient student, followed all orders and tried to learn as much as possible. He was still doubtful about whether he would be able to pull it off, but since he did not wish to disappoint Vivek, he did everything meticulously.

Vivek, on the other hand, was mightily impressed with Paresh's grasping powers. He appreciated the hard work being put in by Paresh and knew that, if given ample time and the right kind of training, he could easily pass him off as a foreign-bred gentleman. But that was a goal for the distant future; for now, his focus was on the Saturday lecture and he wished for it to go off flawlessly.

On Friday, Vivek took Paresh with him to buy a new pair of trousers and a shirt. Although Paresh protested and told him that he already had clothes that he took out during special occasions, Vivek refused to listen to him and went ahead and bought not only the planned items but also a new pair of shoes, a tie, a belt and a cotton suit jacket. All through, Paresh kept telling Vivek that there was no need for him to spend so much on him, as he could manage with whatever clothes he had, but Vivek, who knew the art of making an impression through clothes, did not bother to listen to Paresh's entreaties. Happy with his purchases, he told Paresh that, at the end of the day, the students wouldn't only praise him for his lecture but also the way he looked and presented himself. Paresh was still nervous and not very confident in himself. He just smiled weakly at Vivek. They both then returned home and got on with the last-minute preparations for the big day.

Finally, the fateful day arrived. Both Vivek and Paresh got up with a feeling of anxiety deep in their hearts. Vivek, because he had all his hopes pinned on Paresh; it was his big introduction to the world outside. He wanted Paresh to use this opportunity to make a stir in the industry and show them that anyone could make it big provided he or she had the right attitude. Paresh, on the other hand, was scared, as he did not know what to do. He felt as if all the days of training had been washed out of his head and that he was going to make a fool of himself in front of thousands of students. He wanted to run away to a place where no one could find him. He wanted to be left alone. He wanted time to stand still and not move an inch. He just wanted to skip the lecture at any cost. The first thing he did in the morning was ask Vivek, "*Babuji*, are you still sure that I'll prove to be a safe bet for you? I mean, do you think all this is really necessary? I have a feeling that something might go wrong, so you shouldn't really depend on me for this one. And I also think that you're the best person for the job."

Vivek took a deep breath, as he did not want the day to start on a sore note, and said, "Paresh, listen to me carefully. A lot depends on you today. The world out there wants to meet you, talk to you, listen to you. Not me. I'm no one to them. The vision, the inspiration, the motivation, it's all you. They want you to guide them! You can't be so selfish as to not give in to their demands and just stay away because you think you won't be able to speak. Even if you falter, they won't mind it. That's the beauty of being successful! The moment you reach that level, no matter how good or bad you are, how educated or uneducated, you're accepted with all your frailties. Besides this, you are a good man and an honest one, so you have nothing to fear. You have to rise to the occasion and prove yourself worthy of all this adulation. You have fought so many battles in life, and much bigger ones than this one. You aren't the kind to give in so easily. Just face this day like any other day and enjoy your moment!"

Vivek's words worked like an elixir of sorts on Paresh. He was motivated to do better and take everything in his stride. Charged up, he went to get ready for the momentous occasion. When he stepped out, he was looking dapper and every inch the businessman the world thought him to be. Since it was a big occasion for the family and a rather auspicious one, Neelu gave both Vivek and Paresh a spoonful of curd and sugar as part of a ritual. Divya came to pick both of them up and drop them to the railway station. They were to take a plane from Ahmedabad and so they had to catch an early morning train from Ankleshwar to Ahmedabad. On their way to the station, they stopped at the local temple and sought the blessings of the local deity. Happy and chirpy, they boarded the flight.

Paresh saw an aircraft up close for the first time that day. He felt intimidated by it. Stepping inside was altogether a different experience for him. His eyes popped out with excitement and awe. He did not understand how such a heavy mass of metal could stay afloat up in the air. He was astonished to see smartly dressed women serving food. Until now, for the train journeys he had been on, Neelu had generally packed food in advance or else he and his family would buy food from the railway vendors wherever the train stopped. But, here in the aircraft, everything was served to the passenger. All one had to do was to press the bell and a woman would appear; you placed your request, and your work was done. It all seemed so relaxed to Paresh: a place where things moved smoothly. There were newspapers and magazines to read and small packaged water bottles one could have unlimited servings of; and all these for free. Impressed with the interiors and the fact that he was flying high in the air, he decided that if he went on a holiday with his family, he would take them on an airplane.

They touched down in Pune in the early afternoon. Their lecture was scheduled for four in the evening, so they had close to two hours before it. The secretary of the institute had himself come to receive them at the airport. After the usual introductions, he took them to the hotel first, where they were to stay for a night. Paresh had never seen a five-star hotel from inside, having never stayed in one in his life. The luxury it displayed took Paresh completely by surprise. He had been unaware of such luxuries in life until now. He realized that the world was indeed a big place and one had to explore it to know what it could offer you. He felt happy that he had come to this new city and had two important experiences. First, the experience of sitting in an aircraft and, second, stepping inside a five-star hotel. However, he did not like the exorbitant prices of everything inside the hotel and he stayed away from ordering tea or coffee, as he thought it would be sheer waste of money when one could easily have a better cup at a tea stall outside at a fraction of the price. After lunch, organized by the institute, the two changed into a new pair of clothes and headed for the institute along with the secretary. On their arrival, they were greeted by hordes of media personnel, students and important dignitaries of the institute.

Paresh had never seen such hustle and bustle around him before. He had believed until now that such adulation was meant for movie and sports stars. He had thought that they deserved all the love of people, but finding himself in a situation like that, he was totally flummoxed. He did not know what was so important about him that everyone present in the room wanted their share of fame through him, either by speaking with him or by posing for photographs with him. Even though he was unaffected by the attention at a fundamental level, he felt a little uneasy with all the people trying to 'get a piece' of him. Somehow, they managed to cross the hurdle of people who were thronging the entrance and reached the Dean's office. There again, they were both greeted by a mass of people, but this time in a more organized manner. After posing for dozens of photos, shaking hands with every one present in the room, and garlanded over a thousand times, Paresh softly requested Vivek to allow him a minute to himself before the lecture. Vivek whispered to the secretary that they wanted to be left alone for 15 minutes, which the secretary happily agreed to. Everyone was asked to leave the room and Vivek and Paresh were the only ones left.

"*Babuji*, I just don't know what to do. All this has left me so exhausted. I'm again nervous, and, with so many cameras around, I just don't know what to do."

"Paresh, first of all, stop calling me *babuji*. My name is Vivek and it'd be good if you addressed me like that," Vivek said sternly.

"But, *babuji*, how can I address you by your name? How can I commit such a sin?"

"Come on, Paresh, you're no more the *samosa* maker that I met for the first time on the train. A lot has changed since. You're a big man today. In fact, you're bigger than me in status and your calling me *babuji* doesn't seem right. Not in public at least. So stop it and call me Vivek."

"But—!"

Vivek put a finger to his lips, indicating to Paresh that he was to keep his mouth shut. "Concentrate on yourself for some time and focus on what you're supposed to say minutes from now. Channelize your energy into thinking about your lecture, don't waste it on such trivial issues. You have a big job coming up, so please stay focused."

Paresh sat numbly, with nothing to say. His mind went blank and all he could think about was how he could still end up doing something weird and how he could prevent that from happening. But he soon realized that there was no escaping his predicament and he would have to go through with it, unwillingly. Ten minutes later, a man stepped into the room and whispered something in Vivek's ears.

Vivek then told Paresh, "Time to go, Paresh. The stage is set and the students and media are waiting for you."

While walking towards the auditorium, Vivek whispered into Paresh ears once again, "Don't worry about anything. Just go for it. All the best! And always remember that no matter what the world thinks of you, I'm always standing behind you, ready to take it all."

Paresh was a nervous wreck as he climbed onto the stage. Never in his life had he seen so many people gathered to see him. He could see the cameras pointed at him and that made matters worse. He asked someone to get him a glass of water to calm his nerves but it didn't help much. After he was given a very impressive introduction by the Dean, he was called upon to speak to the audience. He took a few seconds to get up from his chair and then walked towards the mike. That walk was the longest and scariest of his life but he managed it with his head held high. He took out a sheet of paper from the pocket of his jacket and began reading nervously from it.

The Birth of a Phoenix

The fateful day had arrived. Paresh and Vivek were at the venue. Paresh might have had some doubts about himself, but Vivek had none.

When Paresh was introduced to the students, they clapped thunderously. They had found out all about him and his accomplishments on Google. In their eyes, he was the very embodiment of someone whose native wisdom was now a global phenomenon.

Paresh began reading from his prepared text: "Most respected Vice Chancellor and members of this prestigious institution and other honorable guests, and above all, my young friends, the students of the university, my *namaste* and good wishes to you."

Everyone in the auditorium clapped for several minutes.

Paresh continued: "I'm a very ordinary man. There was once a time when I was just a small *samosa* vendor. My small sweets shop was very popular in my small town because of its different kinds of *samosas* and chutneys. I'd learned the art of making *samosas* from my parents. When I took over the shop, I just wanted to earn enough to take care of my family. I didn't have any kind of vision or big dreams. I was incapable of looking beyond a certain limit."

Paresh paused. He appeared to be organizing his thoughts. They were all looking at him expectantly. He quietly put away the papers in his hand and began speaking extempore.

"However, things changed in my life when my friend Vivek, my *babuji*, came into my life. He was the one who forced me to see the immense potential in my *samosas* and the result is our brand today—Matru ka Samosa. Its overwhelming popularity is proof that people have accepted and acknowledged the excellence of the brand.

"Here I must point out to you very categorically that a brand is created after sweating for years and the excellence behind it comes from an overriding will to satisfy the customer. A successful brand today might have a very humble beginning. My own life was very humdrum once. Some of you might start your own business in the coming years. My advice to you is to never, ever be afraid of having your own dreams. There is never a lack of opportunities in life. You must have the eye to select the right opportunities for yourself."

Vivek observed how everyone present in the auditorium was listening to Paresh with rapt attention. Vivek was amazed at Paresh's charisma and newfound confidence.

"My dear friends, today this country is on the threshold of a new business culture and philosophy that are flourishing under dynamic leadership."

"Are you talking about Skill India, sir?" shouted someone from the gathering.

"Yes, I am," answered Paresh in a calm voice.

"Could you clarify what you mean by that?" asked someone else.

Paresh smiled and said, "I thank you for your question. Skill India opens up new ways of addressing the issue being discussed here."

"How?" someone asked.

Paresh's smile broadened. "Had it not been so, how would I be here before you today? After all, I was just an ordinary *samosa* maker!"

There was thunderous applause. Before anyone could ask another question, the anchor intervened and told the audience to stop interfering while the honorable guest was speaking. "My dear friends, please be patient. There will be a question-and-answer session at the end of his speech."

After the brief interruption, Paresh spoke with more confidence. "Dear friends, over the years I've realized that the world is a big place with infinite possibilities. Our country has all kinds of untapped riches. It's a land of opportunities for the many people from aboard who come here in search of art, literature, dance, music, yoga, medicinal cures and a number of other exotic things. Take full advantage of these opportunities. But remember one thing. You get the best in life when your avocation becomes your vocation. This is the ideal situation in life for a person; it generates the greatest happiness." Paresh stopped briefly to study the reaction of the gathering. He felt happy that his audience was listening to him with rapt attention. He resumed. "Let us never ever be ashamed of our culture, our native grandeur, and let us never forget that the world worships innovators. The truth is, a man's originality is his biggest asset in the world; your novelty and inventiveness is the key to your success. Once you begin looking for ideas, they're sure to come to you. In my view, the greatest miracle of human life is its unpredictability. Be a thinking person; don't let your mind rust and fall into a comatose state.

"Your success is measured by your will to step out of watertight compartments in life. By standing on firm ground of your own making, you'll be on your way to winning the world. This country needs men and women like you today. I'm convinced that people of your kind are full of dreams and also have the guts to pursue them. My advice is to never be afraid of your convictions. If anyone is successful, I feel, it's only their self-belief that gets them there.

"Friends, what I'm now going to tell you is of paramount importance. I'm neither a philosopher nor a profound thinker. I'm an entrepreneur and I do business. That's all. Yet, there are moments when I feel that an altruistic approach towards life cannot be overlooked altogether. It's the plinth of humanity. So, never, ever overlook the demands of humanity. We become successful and life becomes meaningful only when our efforts have been of use to others; we're all going to pay for our sins here in this life itself. Afterlife is perhaps just a utopian thought. Who knows if one is going to be reborn? So, why not try and better ourselves in this life only? Shouldn't we help others have a better life? This isn't a sermon. When you become resourceful in life you become a prop—wherever and whenever possible—to poverty-stricken talent. That will give you happiness and make life meaningful. This is our cultural legacy and it must be handed over to posterity." He looked at his audience, trying to read their minds. He felt vibrant within. "Life is the greatest school for a sensitive learner. Situations change, but through good times and bad, I've learned that one should never lose faith in oneself. Self-belief is the key to winning against all odds, so, always trust your own being, your own impulse, and never be defeated by the hostile interventions of life. Only a loser bows down to pressures. Whether they're mental, physical or any other kinds of pressures, walk with your head held high. Every fight must make you stronger. Life consists of challenges, not of endless serendipities. Approach your life in the right frame of mind. Life is short; make the best use of it. Time flies; be creative to the core. Never hold on to resentment against someone you don't like. Acceptance of all situations and all people is the secret of a healthy mind and happiness. That is my motto. It can be yours too."

He stopped. He stood before his audience in his full glory. They felt as if they had been listening not just to a successful businessman but to a *sacer vates*. He had given them the quintessence of life in those valued moments. His words were sacred. All of them stood up and clapped for several minutes.

The audience came alive again at the opportunity to ask questions. As their hands shot up, Paresh took them on one by one, with a lot of patience.

"What's your success formula, sir?" asked one student

"Hard work! Just hard work and a smidgen of luck," said Paresh.

"Can everyone be as successful as you are? I run a grocery shop but I haven't managed to make it big in life," asked another member of the audience.

"It might be the case that you don't love your work and you're carrying on under some compulsion," said Paresh.

"You're right. My dad forced me into doing it. I wanted to go in for theatre," said the man in a sad voice.

"Do we have to have lots of money to begin an enterprise?" asked a student.

Paresh laughed and said, "I don't think so. I began mine with very little investment initially. However, you do require a lot of humility."

A man with an aquiline nose got up. He looked like he was about 30 years old. He said, "Congrats! You delivered a brilliant lecture."

"Thanks!" said Paresh. "What's your question?"

"Don't you think that the present government has done great harm to the small businesses? I feel it has subverted the entire market!" said the man.

"Please don't ask political questions. You shouldn't forget that our guest isn't a politician," someone warned the questioner.

Paresh, looking composed, said, "A question is a question. Let him ask anything." Then, turning towards the person, he asked, "Do you have a business of your own?"

"No, I'm a journalist."

"I'm sorry to tell you that you don't seem to have any idea about real business," said Paresh coolly but with confidence.

"I'm an M.Com," said the man in an offended tone.

"Never mind," said Paresh in an even tone. "I'll explain it to you. In my view, the system emerging in the business world today calls for absolute transparency. Because of it, some people, who have been indulging in dubious deals, are on edge and uncomfortable. My dear friend, a structural change in the market economy, a systemization of our market at all levels from production to sales, is what we need right now."

"Don't you think that Digital India is just an empty, misleading slogan?" someone asked.

"No, I don't think so."

"How do you defend your stand? I feel it has reduced the market to a shambolic state," the questioner persisted in a challenging tone.

Paresh smiled. "I say it from my own experience. I'm not a very educated person. In the beginning, I too was very intimidated by the word 'digital.' Although I had the direction and guidance of my friend Vivek, I wanted to understand everything myself. Today, I'm very comfortable with it. My dear, new modalities cannot be resisted and shunned for too long. Today, this country is changing from a cash economy to a digital one. I feel it'll put an effective check on all kinds of corrupt practices and on evasion of taxes."

"What is your view on expansion of business and branding?" asked a student.

Paresh looked at him kindly. He said, "My dear friend, I've already said something about it in my talk. But since you've asked, I'm going to explain it further. Business should be expanded phase-wise. So should a brand. It follows a snowball process. A continuing effort can result in miraculous results. As you move along with it, new elements get integrated into it automatically, and the business grows."

"Sir, I don't think there are many things to do in business for a newcomer," said a student sadly.

"No, you're wrong. I'm pained to hear that," said Paresh. "There isn't any dearth of ideas and pursuits for a true aspirer. If you diversify by changing a specific consumer item into a different product, then you earn more profit. Even simple *khadi* and jute can be sold in the form of fashionable shirts, ties, *saris* and many other items. I'll give you an example. You design a *sari* made of *khadi* or jute, in tricolor. Market it for Independence Day or Republic Day every year for women living in India and Indian women living abroad. Just see how you sell thousands of *saris* and make good amounts of money because everyone carries that patriotic fervor and expresses it, especially on those chosen days. Like that, there are thousands of ideas you may grow big with in today's world, but only if you make anything and everything into a brand. Be observant and you'll get your ideas."

A very flamboyantly dressed student got up and said, his tone very sarcastic, "Do you mean to tell us that, after getting this degree from this prestigious university, we should sell tea or pull a rickshaw?"

Paresh fixed his gaze upon the questioner. His eyes were full of pity for the young man. His face expressed his feelings when he began answering. "Young man, I feel pity for you, for your attitude. By looking down at certain kinds of jobs, you're only destroying your own possibilities of expansion and growth. Some of the biggest trend-setters in the world started their life's journey from scratch. The list is very long. Take it from me that what seems to be a local product today may grow into a global craze in the future. In this democratic country, every resourceful person has a chance of making it big and being successful. Today, nothing is beyond the reach of a fertile imagination. Let ideas be your treasure."

Vivek observed intently how Paresh was the very image of confidence when answering questions thrown at him by these ambitious young men and women. Although some questions were random, they expressed a willingness to learn and the inclination on the part of the questioners to march ahead of others. In that moment, Vivek felt that some revolution had already begun taking place silently in the country. Expansion and a complete change in the lifestyle of the people were bound to follow. The eagerness of the audience members to learn the magic formula from a successful business magnate was an indication of a more dynamic era in the life of a nation that had been exploited for centuries.

"Can everyone be successful, sir?" a young man asked Paresh.

Vivek was brought back to the present.

Paresh answered, "Yes, it's possible in my view. Why do you doubt it, young man? What I appreciate most in the youngsters of today is that they have been at least thinking about the possibilities. I feel that our creativity has a pragmatic aspect, too."

"Would you elaborate, sir?" asked a smart girl from the audience.

"Pragmatism is a new concept and it must be understood properly. Think of life's possibilities and you'll be surprised. Business is everywhere. There are countless young professionals who don't get any time in the morning for breakfast. A pack of *samosas* with brown bread can solve that problem—make it nutritious and highly enjoyable and you win the hearts of your clients. If you want to, you can provide *idli*, *poha*, *upma*, two stuffed *parathas* or any other such thing. You just have to create 100 such customers initially. You have to provide a fresh and hot breakfast just 15 minutes before their departure for work, so that they can enjoy the breakfast in an Ola or Uber or their private vehicle. That'll help in three ways. It'll get you some money. It'll generate employment. And, above all these, it'll be conducive to the health of the people."

Paresh was cut short by another girl from the gathering. "Creativity is generally considered to be something abstract," she said.

Paresh said, "Considering creativity something abstract is the wrong approach. In fact, creativity can very well be put into a concrete and commercially viable form. My dear friends, what you, as students, are doing here is translating your ideas into generating business. In my opinion, a successful business is always based on a pragmatic philosophy. Business and money are synonymous. At a subtle level of interpretation, they're one and the same thing. A business that doesn't generate resources, that is to say, money, is doomed from the beginning. The phrase 'pragmatic creativity' is related to the concept of producing services and facilities in day-to-day life. Let it be an essential philosophy of young India."

"My question is for Vivek sir," said a young man from the crowd.

"Yes?"

"There is a dearth of jobs in our country today. Unemployment is at an all-time high! What can a qualified person do under such trying circumstances? There aren't enough jobs for the young and qualified lot today! It's the bitter truth!"

"Yes," echoed a number of young students in unison.

Vivek looked at them pensively. "You feel there is unemployment here? There aren't enough job opportunities today? Who gave you these ideas?"

"The newspapers and TV channels are full of news on this," said another young man, somewhat puzzled.

"The opposition has been referring to it vociferously every day," said another voice from the audience emphatically.

"Every day there are protests and marches in one or the other part of the country," said someone else.

"The overall reaction of the youth is unanimous and very clear!"

"I think the government has failed completely in this regard. I feel I'll become an activist in times to come," a young girl said excitedly, looking proudly at others.

"Vivek sir, we all want to hear your views regarding the lack of job opportunities," said a somber-looking youth. He was joined by many others.

Vivek did not begin speaking immediately. *They have raised a vital issue*, thought Vivek. There were people who had been drumming this news constantly into the ears of the public. Those very people who were looked up to— professors, perceptive media persons, business honchos, thinkers and philosophers—were critical of the system and government policy and painting a dark picture of the country. Many subscribed to their pessimistic viewpoint. Vivek did not care a hoot for this view. He was reminded of what an internationally-renowned economist had said about India and how he had painted a dismal picture of the country of his origin. He was a misguided and West-oriented economist who had put on a false mantle of greatness by criticizing the government. Vivek had strongly disagreed with his view.

Finally, Vivek said, "Your observations have shocked me!"

"Why?"

"Because this isn't the truth," said Vivek loudly and emphatically.

This resulted in a medley of questions from the audience.

"How do you mean?"

"We're confused."

"Have those guys been telling lies?"

"Tell us how you look at it."

Slowly, but with the utmost confidence, he said in an assuring tone, "My dear young friends, you're about to enter life's challenging arena. So it's obligatory for you to approach it with a sense of pragmatic creativity. What I want to impress upon your mind today is that there has never been in human history such a big scope for jobs."

The answer still flummoxed them. "Please explain it more clearly to us, sir."

Vivek continued, "Today, human beings are thinking of setting up colonies on other planets. Every day, humans are exploring new regions, searching for new opportunities. In my view, this age and the future belong to the young. They're the ones who are going to set up a new order for mankind. So, my dear young friends, be enterprising. Never, ever be afraid of committing mistakes and learning from those mistakes. Don't back down from any kind of novelty. Even if you're doing something conventional, you can think about doing it in a new style, a new way. If you do that, you'll find innumerable opportunities opening up for you."

"Sir, I have a thought on my mind and I want an honest answer from you," said a girl from the gathering.

"Yes, young lady. You can ask the question," said Vivek.

The girl had bright eyes. They suggested intelligence. Hesitantly, she said, "Today, Paresh sir is such a successful person. Don't you think if you hadn't been there, he wouldn't have attained this height? Isn't it because you are an IITian and a management expert that you could take Paresh sir to his present height?"

Vivek was a bit taken aback by the question, but he answered with full conviction. "Let me be very clear. You've perceived it from an entirely wrong perspective. Paresh sir is a very unique person. I was lucky to have come in contact with him at a time in my life when I'd fallen into the darkest mental instability. At that time, he was the one who propped me up, so to speak, and taught me the art of living. He restored my stability. Later, I saw the hidden drive and vision in him. I merely convinced him to come forward and expand his business."

"So, you brought about a change in his life through his *samosas*," someone said sarcastically.

Everyone burst into laughter. Vivek did not laugh.

"What do you wish to imply by that statement of yours, young man?" asked Vivek sharply.

The questioner was short-statured and obese. He had a bored look in his eyes. In a slightly hostile tone, he said, "We're the management students of this prestigious institution. We don't talk about *samosas* and other eatables here."

Coolly, Vivek responded. "We've gathered here to talk about business management. Don't you think the *samosa* is a part of the food industry? True business lies in seeing and creating opportunities that myopic adventurers don't see. I'd like to categorically suggest to you that you refrain from looking down upon anything, any person or any given chance, if you have the makings of a true business person. Never, ever forget that some of the biggest business setups had the humblest of beginnings. Giants like Google, Apple, Reliance, KFC and many more had very humble beginnings initially. A big business is a big dream, a big vision, and most importantly, a willingness to put in endless effort. The best thing for you is to explore your own inner being. It'll make clear to you what you really want out of your life."

"I want to ask Paresh sir something now," said a girl, her eyes full of curiosity.

"What's your question?" asked Paresh.

"Sir, you're a big name now! Who do you give credit to?"

"Obviously, to Vivek."

"Sorry! I don't accept it," said Vivek, cutting in. "This is not true. The most you can say is it was the union of two elements—his skill in the making of the product and my skill and experience in creating a popular brand."

"But, sir, everyone cannot create a brand out of a product," someone said doubtfully.

"I think everyone can."

"How?"

"What's the most important thing in the making of a brand?" asked Paresh.

"I'm not sure, you tell us," said the girl.

Paresh said, "According to me, the product is the most important thing in the success of a brand. Before one presents any product to one's customers, one should be proud of it first. Secondly, one must maintain its specific quality at all times. Once the people accept it, it becomes a brand. The range of a brand has several categories. It may be local, it may be national or it may be international. Matru ka Samosa was a well-known product in its area. I saw the possibility and transformed it into a global brand. But one thing is very clear. Your product should be capable of winning the trust of your customers."

They were all looking very happy and convinced by now.

Paresh added, "My dear future young entrepreneurs, your product will be your life and will stand for all your moral and ethical values. A business based on venal and corrupt practices cannot survive in a world of values. You must have observed how some of the well-known brands in this country were shorn of their sheen and reputation. Their owners had to flee from the country and from the law. So, I tell you with conviction, and based on my experience, that a brand is the acceptance of your entire being by your trusting customers."

"Vivek sir, I'm a little doubtful about getting the right chance," said a student.

"Be a bold and adventurous practitioner of business, and all things will fall into a pattern," said Vivek, looking at her kindly. She continued looking at him questioningly. He explained, "Identify your clients and their needs and you're on the path to making a brand and a corporate. How? I'll tell you. Let's take an example. There is a great clientele for fresh vegetables. So, you buy fresh vegetables from the *mandi* and put them in attractive packages. It should be a thoughtfully worked-out mix of several kinds of packaging: 15 kg vegetables or, perhaps, one kilo each of potato, tomato, *karela*, beans, onion, *bhindi*, *tori*, *ghiya*, etc. In the *mandi*, most of the vegetables are sold for less than Rs. 20 per kg. So, now, what costs you Rs. 300 overall can be sold for Rs. 500 because you have put them into clearly demarcated, attractive packages. After deducting expenses like cartage, packaging, and the amount spent on procuring an order for, say, a 15-kg pack of different fresh vegetables, you shall save Rs. 100 per customer. If you are able to supply this to 100 customers daily, you are able to make a profit of Rs 10,000 everyday. And soon, these hundred customers get multiplied geometrically. Once you get regular customers for your vegetables, you can expand your business by supplying pulses, spices, pickles, fruits, dry fruits, etc. There are innumerable opportunities and many products in the market to choose from.

"People's psyches have undergone a complete change. What I love most in a young person today is that he or she is not unwilling to experiment and try out new things. There was been a change in the lifestyle of the youth all over the world. They spend their earnings willingly on entertainment, food items, clothes and health items. There is a big market everywhere for brands of all kinds. There is a huge opportunity to make brands out of our handicrafts, cutlery, paintings, icons etc. In this regard, India is the richest country. You can tie up with any famous roadside food outlet and make it a brand by opening more outlets in different places. My view is, whatever is youth-oriented and approved of by the youth will be accepted by all and is going to set the trend in the world and in business. The youth of this country is its greatest treasure. The political setup at present promises a very bright future for creative and enterprising persons. We on the verge of the greatest take-off. The country is now marching towards becoming a global power. Today's world belongs to those young people who're willing to take on risks."

When he stopped, everyone clapped and the sounds of their applause resounded in the auditorium.

Reaching the Summit

After the applause and mandatory goodbyes from the people of the institute, Paresh and Vivek returned to their hotel room. Neither spoke a word to each other during their journey from the institute to the hotel. Vivek was too overwhelmed by the response Paresh had generated and wanted to soak in that feeling for some time.

Paresh, on the other hand, was under the impression that Vivek was angry with him because he had not read the speech he was supposed to. He thought had had faltered big time by speaking nonsense.

Scared that Vivek would admonish him, Paresh, out of fear, said, "I'm sorry. I know the blunder I committed. I should have gone with the plan and read the speech. I don't know why I didn't just do that. I went blank standing there at the podium. I could feel my memory being wiped of everything that you had taught me and told me to say. I did take the paper out of my pocket but just couldn't read from it, as if something had possessed me. I just went on and spoke whatever came to my mind at that time."

As usual, out of nervousness, Paresh was fumbling and blabbering without thinking about whether there was actually a need for him to feel apologetic. Vivek got up from his bed, walked up to Paresh and, holding his shoulders, he said, "You were just too good. I wasn't speaking to you all this while not because I was angry but because I couldn't believe that was really you speaking. I think that the idea of a written and rehearsed speech was bad because whatever you spoke was directly from the heart and nothing could be better than that. Paresh, you have made me really proud today and I cannot express how happy I am at this very moment! You have proved not just to me, but to the entire world today what you're made of and are capable of doing. You don't need anyone now to help you with anything. You're a genius and your capabilities exceed anyone's. I have just one request for you. Remain how and what you are. Do not change with time because your simplicity is your greatest asset and I wish to always see you the way you are right now."

Paresh's eyes welled up with tears. He had never had anyone say such kind words to him. To him right now, the world outside did not matter. He did not care what power he wielded in the world then. The words of the person who had made him the man he was now mattered the most to him and, now that Vivek had put his stamp of approval on him, Paresh felt as if he had attained nirvana. He was beaming with joy. He had attained his greatest achievement to date and he wanted the world to know that.

Even though his heart was choked with emotions, Paresh managed to say to Vivek, "Can I also ask you for a favor and hope you won't refuse me this one last time?"

"Of course, Paresh, you can ask me anything and you know I'll never refuse," said Vivek.

"Can I continue calling you *babuji*?"

Vivek broke into laughter and said, "If you wish to."

***

The early morning June sun brought radiance and warmth to Divya's face. The sheer brightness of it pleasantly surprised her for a moment. "If the mirror could speak, it would have certainly expressed bafflement at the new glow," Divya told herself. But in her heart of hearts she knew the reason. It was the early morning news! Ramu *kaka* brought in the usual "*bitia, aap ki chai*" along with the day's newspaper. Taking the first sip of the warm tea, and loving the aroma of Darjeeling's moist soil, she blinked as her eyes took in the big, bold headline on the front page—"Matru ka Samosa: The Hot, Spicy New Indian Dream." She felt the power and punch in the headline could wake the whole nation up. She sat up and devoured each word.

Soon she discovered that the story, written more like a features article, was like a high-energy breakfast, not just for the hunger of the ambitious but also a large shot of espresso to wake up the dormant ones. Everything about it was upbeat—the dream, the hope, the power, the confidence, the determination; and above all, the new Indian pride. It talked about the new age ethos and mindset, about how, slowly, the spirit of enterprise was getting into the "*youngistan*" psyche. It also talked of the opportunities that lay ahead for everyone if the nation embraced this positive, progressive and adventurous mindset. It spoke at length about the possibilities of wealth creation and also of breaking the inhibitions that could stand in the way of an enterprising outlook. It profusely applauded the vision of Vivek and Paresh—one an IITian, the other a simple *samosawala*, and together the spark for a new revolution epitomizing a new age vision and partnership, a model for the nation! The story concluded with a hopeful, "If only the whole nation learned to catch up with the spirit of this vision and partnership fast and if only we saw the new light spread to every corner of the nation."

The last line was a bomb! Divya could feel the light spreading into every corner of her being, energizing every cell inside her. It was as if a positive current was flowing through her, engulfing her fully and brightening her. It was the current of the new Indian dream that made a sleepy Divya suddenly wake up and see a new rainbow on the horizon, filled with all the colors of new dreams and hopes. It was this current that filled her with energy and, suddenly, she felt charged up and fresher than any spring morning. For a moment, she felt thrilled about this wonderful feeling, the new zest and the force in it. The plenty and the fulfillment in it. Not wasting time, she felt like calling Vivek and thanking him for what he and his vision had made possible. But for some unknown reason, instead of reaching for the mobile phone, she stood in front of the mirror. Perhaps to see how happy she was, perhaps to say to herself, "You're a small part of a big change. After all, Vivek said your contribution was a key one. That's how big things get created. They are made to work through countless small and big contributions." She knew that she'd played a part, however small it may have been.

But there was more to follow, of course. Maybe, for some mysterious reason, her subconscious dragged her to the mirror before talking to Vivek. Maybe by thinking of Vivek, she felt his presence around and the woman in her brought her to the mirror to see them together. And then, she blushed. Trying to control it, she went back to bed, sat, took a deep breath and began sipping her tea again. Having achieved a little composure, she reached for the phone, but again halted for a moment.

"What will I say to him anyway?" she asked herself. Just thank him? Tell him to read the news? Read it out to him with the loudest possible voice, so that the world could also hear what Vivek had made possible and know how that had affected her, motivated her? Or, just tell him how her love for him had become what it had—fragrant spring on a summer morning—and that only he could be given credit for his philanthropic attitude and his drive for social good!

Those were too many thoughts together, too much to handle. Divya thought of lying in bed for a while more. "He could be sleeping!" The decision to just sit back and remain focused on doing nothing brought her thoughts back to the dream that refused to leave her. So she dreamt, with her eyes wide open.

Epilogue

Life is the greatest enigma. It is unpredictable. For some, it is a sacred odyssey, while for others it is mere drudgery. Everything in life depends on how one approaches it, the consequences of our thought process included. A panoramic view of life is a rare phenomenon. Only the bold and adventurous souls of the world come by secret treasures.

Who is a real hero in life? It is a mind-boggling question. It cannot be answered casually. This is so because it calls for a headlong dive into the depths of life. Only a rugged and fighting soul, one who can bear the brunt of life sportingly, can tell you how beautiful human existence is! From time immemorial, there have been inventive persons who have added to the beauty of our existence and have expanded the reach of our awareness.

Once, Vivek had gone for a big gathering of his old friends from IIT and IIM, organized at the Tughlaq Road residence of one of his classmates, Suresh Kumar, in New Delhi. Suresh was a senior IFS officer with the Government of India. Many of his classmates had acquired high positions in life. There were some in-service big administrators and also some retired ones. Among the guests were the High Commissioner of Mauritius and the Ambassador of France. Suresh was introducing Vivek to everyone present and apprising them of his work, especially his social work in villages, which was the talk of the country then. All of the people gathered there were congratulating Vivek for it.

The High Commissioner of Mauritius in India said to Vivek, "I haven't just come here to congratulate you for your social work."

"What have you come here for then, my dear friend?" asked Vivek, surprised.

"For Matru ka Samosa. I, too, have sampled the delicious *samosas* here in India, and now I want to make them popular in my country too."

Some of them said together loudly, "Yes, we'll make MKS popular all over the world."

"It's becoming a global brand now," said someone.

"It's a great snack," said the Ambassador of France in India, biting into his *samosa.*

Vivek was lost in thought with a glass of wine in his hand, wondering how the world had changed for him in the last 10 years. He had gone from being a frustrated man who wanted to run from the world to being appreciated throughout the country and the world for his venture. The credit for this he always gave to Paresh, his mentor. He was, however, clear in his mind that he had to dedicate his life to the upliftment of the poor and improving the condition of the villages in the country. He owed that to the nation and the institutions that had made him capable of bringing change to the lives of the people of India.

***

"Memories are powerful. They suddenly rush by, Divya. One cannot smother them at will. You have to accept them. Live with them, whether bitter or sweet. Now I feel completely relaxed, Divya," Vivek said to Divya at home.

Smiling at him, she said, "The credit ought rightly to be given to Paresh. Weren't you a very disturbed soul when you met him for the first time?"

"It seems his equanimity and fortitude have their provenance in strength of the heart," Vivek said. "Divya, I'll let you in on a secret today."

"Do you still have secrets?" asked Divya humorously.

"Yes, I have one."

"Share it with me, then."

"I will."

"I'm now burning with curiosity."

"I don't have much faith in people's views."

"Why?"

"I feel they're just a crowd."

"What makes you feel so harshly about collective opinion?"

"I have my own reasons."

"I know your reasons."

"Really?"

"Yes, but tell me if you care to. I don't think you can convince me, though," she said with her characteristic spunk.

"I can," he said emphatically.

"Go on."

He did not say anything for several moments. She waited patiently.

"All outside observers who know us think that I have been a prop to Paresh and that's the greatest lie in my view. A lie that they aren't even aware of," he said in one breath.

She was now surprised. She could only ask, "And what's wrong with that viewpoint, Vivek?"

"Divya, it's the biggest lie, believe me!"

"How is it a lie?"

"Before I answer your question, can I ask you what your impression is of Paresh?"

"He's a simple person."

"True, he is that in certain aspects, but, at other levels, he is a most complex guy," said Vivek with utmost conviction.

She said, "You're not being any clearer."

Fixing his gaze upon her, he said, "Divya, the truth is that I have never been a prop for Paresh. Rather, he has been a prop to me!"

This surprised her greatly. "How?" she asked, full of curiosity.

"If he and his family hadn't been there for me in my desperate hours, then I'd have collapsed and perished under the ruthless pressures of the world. Their unconditional love helped me overcome those negative circumstances."

"But you're the one who made him reach these heights of material success," argued Divya.

"That's nothing, Divya."

"How can you say that?"

He explained, "It's very simple. Even if I weren't with him, his family, he…they would have survived happily, but, if I hadn't had that support then, you can't even imagine what my plight would have been."

"Hmm, an interesting way to put it."

"One thing more, Divya."

"What?"

"Paresh is more perceptive and intuitive than me."

She looked at him. "It's becoming tougher now for him," she said.

"Divya, Paresh is a very tough guy and a born fighter. People like him never give up. They're the winners of the world."

Divya's eyes sparkled. "Really? Great!"

Vivek continued, "Our friendship rests on terms of equality. If I've contributed something towards his life, then he, too, has contributed something towards mine." He stopped briefly and then, looking pensively at Divya, added, "I request you to evaluate and appreciate Paresh and his activities from an unprejudiced angle."

"I understand. I'll follow your advice now. Any kind of prejudice results in a narrow evaluation." Divya paused and then said, "Okay, dear, I must go now to attend to some other work. Bye bye!"

Memories kept rushing through Vivek's mind. He smiled at memories of his conversations with Paresh.

"Paresh, we have only four cold storages at present. We're now a big setup. We can in go for some more cold storages," he said to Paresh one day, when they were having tea together.

"I don't question your decision at all. You're the pivot and master in this setup. But, right now I want to ask you, *babuji*, what will you do with extra cold storages? We just store potatoes in them."

Vivek said, "We can store more potatoes in them."

"But, we don't need that many potatoes."

Vivek smiled and said, "It'll fetch a good profit for us."

"How?"

"We buy potatoes when they are cheap, and we sell them as and when the prices go up. That's all. Lots of money comes to us," explained Vivek.

This disturbed Paresh a lot. He kept looking at Vivek fixedly and with a choked voice, he could only say, "Why this?"

Seeing his blank face, Vivek said, "Don't let anything be a burden on your mind, dear Paresh. Say whatever is on your mind."

Reassured, Paresh blurted out, "Won't it be black marketing, *babuji*?"

Vivek guffawed. Holding Paresh's hand into his, he said, his voice reassuringly firm, "My dear Paresh, this isn't black marketeering. Earning profit in business is legal and valid. Whatever we do will be fair and we'll pay the taxes on our profits."

When Paresh left, Vivek thought about how Paresh was a very powerful person because his character was transparent. He also thought about how only a transparent business could bring about true prosperity to an individual and the nation and its people at large. He remembered how he was led into devoting his time to guiding brilliant but poor students towards the fulfillment of their dreams. He was impelled by a voice within him. There were moments when he thought about the possibility of expanding the services that could change the very face of the nation. There were a number of inspired brilliant young men and women from prestigious institutions who devoted themselves wholly to the task of carrying out the mission at a global level.

Memories were good friends in a way.

As he watched the train rattle on the old rails of the small gauge tracks to Shimla, he remembered his train journey 10 years ago. So much had changed. He would be seeing his mother for the first time since then. It felt quite natural to be going there with Divya. She understood him like no one else ever had.

Divya asked Vivek jokingly, "What do you get from your non-commercial activities, Vivek?"

On hearing her words, Vivek became very serious. When he began speaking, his face glowed with conviction. He said, "Divya, remember one thing: that in each brilliant mind, creative mind, there is a national, no, rather, international property. I see the salvation of mankind through it. Besides this, it is a source of true contentment."

When Vivek stopped, Divya noticed that his expression had changed; he was beaming. She felt a deep love for him in that moment. Kissing him impulsively, she said, "My dear Vivek, I see now, rather feel, what you've got on your mind. Right now, I can tell you just this much: that I am there for you all the time. I'm very sure that you've realized your life's dream. The dream of contributing something to the making of the society."

Casting a long, searching glance at her, Vivek said, "Divya, I never expected all these things even in my wildest dreams. When I came here, I was a shattered man: but, now, I'm a man with a mission. I saw here a number of talented boys and girls being forced to lead a miserable life of poverty, all because they couldn't get a proper education. There isn't any dearth of talent in this country. But there is dearth of resources for some."

"I appreciate your concern for the people, for your country," Divya said appreciatively.

Vivek went on, pensively, "I got the idea of creating spaces for the youth of this country. All my numerous institutes and other professional institutions today have been following the principles that I derived from my own experiences over the years. It's my conviction today that the youth of this country is willing to take up every challenge and break new ground for itself. Today, this country is changing. It's preparing itself to create a number of global gurus in different branches of life."

"Why do you look so sad, Vivek? This is the biggest day of your life. You must celebrate it with all of us," said Divya with the utmost warmth in her voice.

"Tell me, dear Divya, how is this the biggest day in my life?"

A smile spread over her face. "It's obvious to everyone."

"But I don't understand. Maybe I'm a dullard."

"Now, you're a celebrity! You are a Padma Shri awardee!" She paused to organize her words, as she wanted them to be more impressive and effective. Vivek just waited patiently, his gaze fixed upon her face. She went on, "It means that people all over this country have begun to appreciate your efforts. In my view, any such appreciation is a vindication of the quality of one's intention and activities."

Divya was looking at him with tenderness in her eyes. Vivek felt a strange sensation course through him. It was always like that when she spoke in that kind of tone. At last, breaking a long silence, he said, "My dear, whatever I have been doing in Divi—my adopted township—is my pattern for the rest of the country, too. I'm happy that there are some who have been enthused by my still inchoate dreams about those unnoticed talents in the rural areas and in other overlooked quarters. This country is today going through a subtle but definitive process of intellectual, social and cultural fermentation. In my mission, I am no longer alone now. A number of IITians and bright young professional from other walks of life want to assist me in creating infrastructure. We don't have any dearth of talents here. But it remains waiting for a chance."

When he stopped, Divya said, "I wish you all success in your great mission. I'm with you in it forever."

His eyes had a strange glow now and he whispered, lost in his own world, "This country has the most potential of any in the world. It can even be a leader in the field of sports. There are countless challenges before us at present but we'll get over them. I want to contribute in my own way towards this silent revolution and be an essential and inseparable part of it, too. The time is ripe for the execution! My mission has become my life now. I want all disadvantaged talents to find a harbor in me. I'll burn myself out. This Padma Shri is just one small step towards a great, idealistic mission."

Divya's eyes moistened in those very private moments. She could now perceive clearly how Vivek had reached a state of selflessness. Instantly, she realized how only selfless service led to the making of a great nation. It was the hardest task for the nation builders to pick out and measure up and meter talents that had been rotting in the absence of opportunities.

Divya's voice mellowed when she said, "Together, we move on to nourish talents everywhere! I hail commander Vivek! What's your order to me, sir? Your most trusted soldier is willing to sacrifice anything! Just give me space in your ship!"

Vivek smiled. Casting a loving glance at her, he said, softly but firmly, "No longer any histrionics, Divya. I cannot think of any mission without you standing beside me. You're the one I can share my most secret ambitions and thoughts with. Do you understand?"

"Yes, commander, I do!" she said, her voice stable and assuring.

For several moments, Vivek did not say anything. Divya kept observing his face intently. She saw how his very countenance suggested his determination to fight. In those moments, she felt as if Vivek was a phoenix who, after having been reborn from his own ashes, was ready to fly into space, carrying the whole world.

"It cannot be delayed any more, Divya!" Vivek's firm voice came floating into her eyes and brought her back to reality. He continued, "It calls for systematic planning. Only then will we be able to generate plans for the fulfillment of our dreams of building up a new world. Our planning should begin from the grassroots level. We must pick out talents from a very early age."

"It's all so absorbing, so promising," Divya said. "Your thought of restructuring the entire process of development is the beginning of a different kind of evolution at several levels of existence. Vivek, this idea of yours has infinite possibilities. Now, give me some assignment too!"

He laughed. "Now, you can't back out from your duties. You had better gird up your loins, my dear! Be ready for our mission!"

"I'm a willing slave."

Vivek then said, "We will spread the network of our activities from the rural areas and try to reach as many people as possible."

Divya cut in, "We can contact people through *gram panchayats.*"

Vivek said, "Exactly! Wherever we see a ray of light, we accept it."

***

They had begun to implement their plans in all sincerity. Vivek and Divya had once gone to address a gathering of administrators on the invitation of the government.

"Ladies and gentlemen, here I have come to you with an appeal. The time has now come to hunt for and discover

257

talents, not just in big cities or among the well-groomed fortunate ones. We must find talents in unknown nooks and unimaginable spots. Our rural world is still unexplored from this angle. I'm sure your contribution towards the evolution of a new India can be immense. It is high time that we step out of the cocoon of our prejudices and accept the truth of life. Since this the age of electronics, we can easily expose this vastly talented but hitherto neglected lot to the different lifestyles, cultures and regions through films and other means. We must show, in every village and in small towns, a number of telefilms on big screens that will expose people to how the world is progressing. Let our children, living in villages or small towns, start dreaming big dreams at an early age. They cannot progress until they have the ambition to fly. It will expand the vision of innocent, eager, energetic and talented youngsters beyond their wildest fancies. A silent, social upheaval is going on in our great, ancient nation. We must now reject the sham culture of exclusivity. Once we begin doing it, we'll have an abundance of talents in different aspects of life. Give life a new definition. Success must be redefined. Vocational training must be made compulsory between Classes 4 and 6. Even if anyone drops out without completing his or her schooling, survival would not be a problem for the drop-out. Right now, a new order is in the making here and all of us present here must give it our profoundest thought. This country is ready for a quantum leap. That is my conviction."

Everyone present burst into thunderous applause. In the evening, sitting over a cup of tea with Vivek, Divya said, "I wonder if you really need me, even though I wish to be with you."

"What are you saying, Divya?" Quickly, he moved forward. He took her into his arms. Then, kissing her forehead, he said, "Nonsense! You're the most valued person here. The rest of the mission, we'll carry out together."

Her face beamed. She threw her arms around Vivek's neck and whispered, "From, today, from this very moment, I'm the partner of a missionary."

Embracing Divya tightly, he whispered, "You're love's biggest gift to me!"

Kissing him warmly, she said, "Today, I've attained true womanhood!"

They were both drowned in radiance as another train journey began; this time, for the two of them.

A Few Years Later...

Vivek and Paresh were sitting together.

"Paresh, do you hear the footsteps of the changing world?" Vivek asked.

"Yes I do, my friend! Although it's muffled, it's there!" said Paresh, somewhat absorbed in his own musings.

"We've now handed over our torch to the next generation and they ought to be given a free hand to carve out their own paths," mumbled Vivek somewhat incoherently.

"The youth will change the world and make it more prosperous and peaceful for everyone," observed Paresh.

"Let business be free from the tyranny of ruthless politics," said Vivek.

"Vivek, my dearest friend, I see a revival of values in life."

"The youth today isn't antagonistic to morality. Give it space to grow. It is the power of the world. Give it encouragement and it'll create its own occupation. When it realizes how there isn't any dearth of jobs, then it will begin looking for its possibilities everywhere," said Vivek with verve.

Paresh and Vivek sat, teacups in hand. Their radiant faces confirmed their happiness.

Acknowledgements

Thoughts are thoughts. They could be ideas, feelings, dreams, directions, visions, missions, simple desires and more. Thoughts must not be locked inside. Instead, they should be allowed to speak and communicate!

I would like to thank:

Shri V. K. Joshi and Ms. Jean Pandian for helping me put this book together with their excellent editing. I am also thankful to Ms. Priya Dubey for having extended her hand with creative inputs, which have been very inspiring and made me a better writer. My deep and sincere thanks to the trio, who did more than I could ever have expected.

Sarthak Jain, an M.S. in Chemical Engineering from Carnegie Mellon University, Pittsburgh, USA, who, despite his busy schedule, still took out time to discuss the issues and problems of young India with me, provided me new-age insights and encouraged me to complete this book.

My niece, Upasna Jain, and my daughter-in-law, Mansi Jain, for whom I have much love, appreciation and admiration. They took printouts, edited, corrected and, above all, reassured me over and over again about my concern and care for young people who fail to find any direction because of unemployment.

About the Author

Pravesh Jain, the CEO of Paras Dyes & Chemicals Pvt. Ltd, takes a huge interest in social service and philanthropic and intellectual activities. His Paras Foundation runs an old age home, a school for street children and an institution for the visually impaired.

Born and educated in Delhi, he has contributed articles and columns to prestigious newspapers over the years. His book *One Mind, Many Thoughts* was brought out by Rupa Publications. The book consists of philosophical musings on diverse aspects of life.

His creative urge finds cogent expression in all his activities and thoughts. He is a dynamic social philosopher. It is his conviction that, to bring about a real change in society, mere philosophy is not enough. It is only possible through a pragmatic approach to everyday issues.

Around the World with Four Samosas is his first work of fiction.